"Three days to plan a wedding!"

"You'll have one day to decide, then we need to go to the county clerk's office to apply for a license. I suggest you call your relatives, friends and business associates tomorrow and make travel arrangements for them. I'll take care of the rest."

Jodie looked completely stunned as she sat upright in the chair, framed by the window. In the dark glass, Travis saw a reflection of the room. He saw himself, looking stiff and determined. Well, fine. That was how he felt. His decision was firm—he wasn't getting married again unless it was for keeps. Maybe he and Jodie didn't have enough in common to build a marriage.

But maybe, just maybe, they did.

Dear Reader,

Ranger Springs, Texas, is the type of place that exists in stories I've heard from my wonderful native-Texan in-laws, Vaughn and Lillian Huffstutler, and in my imagination of what a small town should be. It's the type of place where I'd love to live—if only they had a major mall, a large grocery store and a Starbucks! In that regard, I'm very similar to the heroine of *Coming Home to Texas*, Jodie Marsh. She's a California "city girl" who marries Texas rancher Travis Whitaker. She must then adapt to his adopted hometown in the Texas Hill Country. I'm a Kentucky "city girl" who married my very own Texan thirty-three years ago.

Jodie and Travis Whitaker are modern characters in a traditional setting. She's a plus-size model and he's a famous architect. They are introduced by characters you might recognize from *The Prince's Cowboy Double* and *The Prince's Texas Bride*. Their attraction is immediate— with consequences that extend well beyond the nine months she anticipates.

I hope you enjoy this sixth book in my Ranger Springs series. Please write to me at P.O. Box 852125, Richardson, TX 75085 and include a SASE for reply, or e-mail me at victoriachancellor@msn.com.

Best wishes and happy reading,

Victoria Chancellor

COMING HOME TO TEXAS
Victoria Chancellor

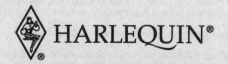

TORONTO • NEW YORK • LONDON
AMSTERDAM • PARIS • SYDNEY • HAMBURG
STOCKHOLM • ATHENS • TOKYO • MILAN • MADRID
PRAGUE • WARSAW • BUDAPEST • AUCKLAND

ISBN 0-373-75039-0

COMING HOME TO TEXAS

www.eHarlequin.com

Printed in U.S.A.

To my lovely niece Laura Madrill, her wonderful
husband, David, and their precious Garrett Adam.
All the best forever.

Thanks to former model and supermother
Cari Manderscheid for her expertise.

Books by Victoria Chancellor

HARLEQUIN AMERICAN ROMANCE
844—THE BACHELOR PROJECT
884—THE BEST BLIND DATE IN TEXAS
955—THE PRINCE'S COWBOY DOUBLE
959—THE PRINCE'S TEXAS BRIDE
992—THE C.E.O. & THE COOKIE QUEEN

Chapter One

Jodie Marsh gathered her courage along with her Kate Spade tote and umbrella, preparing to make a mad dash toward Travis Whitaker's front porch. A mad dash toward her immediate future. With one last sigh, she pushed open the door to her rental car and swung her legs out. Her feet landed in a puddle and she watched as her Manolo Blahnik sandals disappeared in a small pool of muddy water. Great. Now she would squish when she confronted him.

Travis wasn't expecting her and she doubted he'd even heard the car pull into the driveway over the persistent rain. His house looked spacious and new, although it also reminded her of the old rock homes and weathered-wood barns she'd seen dotting the countryside. She assumed he'd designed it since he was an architect.

Jodie stopped on the porch and folded her umbrella, shaking the water from it. Frowning, she wiggled her sandals, but they were still wet enough to make her feet feel slippery. And cold. She'd assumed Texas would be warmer and drier. Now she was mentally and physically uncomfortable. She took another deep breath and peered inside the house.

The windows were dark and looked rather intimidating beneath the leaden sky, but she wasn't going to let rain or her imagination stop her from talking to the man with whom she'd spent one spectacular weekend almost five weeks ago. He'd been a blind date, but a fantastic one. They'd shared an immediate attraction—and much more—for two and a half days in Monte Carlo.

She'd hesitated long enough. After placing a hand on her stomach, she rang the doorbell. And waited.

And waited. Where was Travis? She'd called from the airport but had hung up as soon as he'd answered. Calling had been a mistake. She couldn't talk to him on a crackling, staticky cell phone during a thunderstorm. What she had to say needed to be said in person, so she'd driven here as quickly as possible from the San Antonio airport.

"Where are you, Travis Whitaker?" she whispered as she pressed the doorbell again then added a few knocks in case the electricity was out. The lunch crowd at a quaint diner in downtown Ranger Springs had told her how to find the ranch, and she had to assume he hadn't left in the past hour.

Just when she thought she might have to search elsewhere on the property for the elusive architect, the door flew open.

"Jodie?"

"Hello, Travis." She stared at his disheveled, sunstreaked hair, frayed University of Texas sweatshirt and faded jeans. His beautiful feet were bare. He looked so much like he had just after they'd made wild, passionate love that her heart skipped a beat.

"What are you— Never mind, that was rude, and not what I meant. Please, come inside."

She leaned her umbrella against the house, shook more water from her sandals and slid past him into the warmth of his home. Mmm. He even smelled the same, like clean, warm male and Mediterranean sunshine, despite the rainy, cool Texas day.

"Can I get you something? You look a little cold."

She wasn't about to tell him she was shaking more from nerves than the weather. Instead she shook her head. "I'm fine."

"Come into the great room. I have a fire going."

She followed him down the slate-tiled hallway, her wet sandals slapping against the floor, like a prisoner being led to the gallows. Not that they really used gallows anymore. Not that she'd done anything wrong, or wanted to feel like a criminal…or a victim.

Not that she was so nervous that she was babbling inside her head. With each step, an unaccustomed sense of panic increased until she couldn't stand the tension a moment longer.

"Wait," she said, grabbing his arm as they reached the doorway. "I have something to tell you and I need to do it now, before we get comfortable in front of the fire." Before he made her feel welcome in his home.

"What's wrong?" He looked so handsome, so concerned, as he reached out to steady her. His hands felt strong and comforting on her shoulders, as if he'd reached out to her many times before. As if they'd had more than a couple of fantastic days together.

She wanted to wrap her arms around his neck, to hold him tight and to whisper the truth. But she needed to see his face, not retreat to his warmth and strength, when she broke the news.

"Not quite wrong, but…" she began. "Well, I'm not sure how you're going to react, so I need to just tell you this. Right now, right here."

"What's going on, Jodie?"

She took a deep breath, then the words rushed past her cold, trembling lips. "I'm pregnant. The baby is definitely yours. And we need to get married right away."

He looked as stunned as she'd felt when the doctor had confirmed the pregnancy kit test result. America's new "girl next door" was going to be an unwed mother unless she could get Travis Whitaker's immediate cooperation.

"PREGNANT?" he repeated, dropping his hands from her shoulders and stepping back. His immediate joy that she'd arrived in Ranger Springs, coupled with surprise that she'd sought him out, came to an abrupt halt. He felt as if he'd been poleaxed. Him, a father?

But he shouldn't be all that surprised. They'd used protection all but one time, when she'd surprised him in the shower. He hadn't been prepared for her sexy smile, her slippery, soft skin and very talented use of a body puff. In so many ways Jodie was unlike any other woman he'd been involved with.

"Yes, pregnant," she said. "I know I said we should be okay, that it was a safe time of the month, but apparently I was wrong."

"I—I don't know what to say."

She narrowed her eyes and placed her hands on her curvy hips. "You don't *have* to say anything, but I'm hoping I can get your cooperation. Travis, this is important to me."

"Having a baby is rather important to everyone involved, wouldn't you say?" he asked with barely controlled sarcasm. What did she mean, it was important to *her,* when she'd just dropped a bombshell on *him* and added that they needed to get married right away?

"Look, I know you're shocked and disappointed—"

"With all due respect," he interrupted, running a hand through his shaggy hair, "I don't think you know me well enough to decide what I'm feeling."

She stepped back, turning a little pale beneath her golden, California-girl tan. "Okay, I understand your position. I'd just go away and leave you alone, but—"

"I didn't ask you to leave."

"You don't seem especially glad to see me, either. Which I can understand, given what I just told you."

"I was—am—glad to see you. But you did throw me for a loop. You certainly don't mince words, do you?"

"Not on anything this important."

He ran his hand through his hair again, wishing they could start over. "Look, let's go sit down and talk like reasonable adults. The fire is warm and, quite frankly, you look as though you need to sit down."

"Great. Just the look I was going for—helpless female."

"Jodie, I don't think anyone would call you helpless, or weak, or any other unflattering adjectives. But you are definitely female."

When he'd first met Jodie, he'd been pleasantly surprised. His friends had mentioned she was a model who'd just finished a swimsuit photo shoot in Monaco. He'd been expecting a silicone-enhanced, tall, tanned, self-indulgent, waiflike creature. Not his usual type of petite, acquiescent woman, but heck, he was flexible. What red-blooded American male would turn down a date with a swimsuit model? Then he'd met her in a café in Monte Carlo and he'd immediately known he'd gotten her all wrong.

Jodie wasn't just a swimsuit model. She was a famous model, a minor celebrity. And she wasn't just a regular model. She was a plus-size model. Size fourteen to sixteen, she'd told him over a generous meal of pasta, salad and dessert. She had to eat heartily to maintain her size because she was so active, participating in a variety of sports.

Definitely not the usual dainty, blond and predictable type of woman he preferred to date. His friend Hank McCauley would also add "airhead" to the description, but Travis thought that was an exaggeration. So what if his girlfriends didn't have strong career directions or advanced degrees? He liked women whose jobs didn't interfere with his somewhat erratic work and vacation schedule. He wanted to be able to call someone at the spur of the moment and say, "Let's go to Tahiti."

"All right," she sighed. "Let's sit down and talk this through. Maybe I could use a cup of tea."

"Coming right up. Make yourself comfortable in front of the fire," he said, carefully taking her arm and steering her toward the center of the large house. "I'll be right back."

He gratefully retreated to the kitchen to prepare mugs of Earl Grey, placing them with honey, sugar and artificial sweetener on a tray. He wasn't sure what pregnant women were supposed to drink. About all he knew about pregnancy was that it took nine months and sometimes involved unpleasant morning sickness.

Had Jodie been ill? Is that why she'd paled at his sarcastic comment? He was a heel for upsetting her, but dammit, he sure hadn't been expecting an announcement that she was carrying his child.

He grabbed a couple of spoons and felt a sudden urge to hurry back into the den. One part of him dreaded the upcoming conversation, but another wanted to know every little detail. How she'd learned of the pregnancy. What she was feeling. What were her plans for the baby…and how did they include him?

Marriage? He definitely didn't plan to get married again. Marriage involved messy emotions that led to botched expectations, then disappointments, and finally, crying and yelling. But still, she was pregnant…

"Here you go," he said as cheerfully as possible, placing the tray on his large tufted ottoman. "I hope you like Earl Grey."

"One of my favorites," she said, pushing her shoulder-length blond hair behind her ear. His eyes settled on her neck and he remembered, with a flush of heat, how sensitive she was in that particular spot, just below her ear. He'd felt an enormous sense of possession when he'd kissed her there, hard, as he'd moved inside her.

Shaking away the memory, he straightened and tugged on the hem of his old U.T. sweatshirt. Jodie was sitting in one of the big carved wood and upholstered chairs near the fireplace. He took the other one, then grabbed a mug of tea, searching for a safe way to begin this conversation.

"So, have you been in California?"

"Mostly, although I spent some time in New York City. That's one of the reasons I needed to see you right away. Something has developed in my career."

"Something good?"

"Absolutely. I think I mentioned a possible cosmetics contract last month when we were…well, in Monte Carlo. As soon as I returned, I found out that they want me to become their new image. I signed the contract two weeks ago to become 'the girl next door,' as they call it." Jodie looked away and laughed mirthlessly, a sad sound against the soft crackle of the fire. "Some girl next door. Unless, of course, your neighbor is pregnant and unwed."

"If you've already signed the contract, surely they'll work with you on the ad campaign. Maybe change the timing or just show you from the chest up."

Jodie shook her head. "It's not that simple. The contract has a morality clause. I can't do or say anything that will negatively impact myself or the company while I'm representing them. Keep in mind that I'm supposed to be the *girl next door*, not the jet-setting California tramp."

Ouch. Becoming an unwed mother would probably violate the contract, even with the relaxed morality of big cities as opposed to small towns. "I see your problem."

"It's rather obvious, isn't it? Without your cooperation, I can have my baby or I can have my career." She leaned forward, holding the mug like a talisman. "Well, I want both."

Travis took a deep breath. "I've tried being married, Jodie. I didn't like it."

"Tough. Look, I'm not asking you for eternal love and commitment. I'm asking for your name for our baby, your cooperation in a marriage. A temporary marriage. Perhaps make some appearances with me. Act happy over the baby, that sort of thing. I promise I won't bother you all that much. After all, I'll be pretty busy with my endorsements, assignments and other activities."

"Not to mention the baby."

"Of course. I meant, before the baby is actually born. My agent is quietly working on a deal with a maternity clothing line."

"Sounds like you have it all planned out. Hell, this could be a great break for you." He tried to keep the bitterness out of his voice, but knew he failed. So what? Although life had handed her a basket of lemons, it sounded to him as if Jodie was making lemonade with great gusto. Or maybe she'd been "expecting" these lemons all along. Was he just another part of her plan?

"Everything seems to be coming together for you nicely. All you need is a husband, now that you have the new contract and a baby on the way."

"I didn't plan to get pregnant! I knew nothing about this 'girl next door' campaign the company has planned."

His suspicions must have shown on his face. Travis shrugged. "Still, you got pregnant, and now you're here, demanding my cooperation because of all your contracts and endorsements."

"Hoping for your cooperation," she interrupted, "so I can save my career and support this baby."

"Whatever. All I know is that you claim to be having my baby, but I haven't had any say in your plans."

"This baby is affecting my career, not yours."

"Don't be so sure about that."

"What do you mean?"

He leaned forward, facing her over the edge of the ottoman. "I mean that I live in a small community with traditional values. I don't want my friends and neighbors thinking I'm an irresponsible man or a dead-beat dad. I don't want them assuming I have indiscriminate affairs."

"Oh, so now I'm to blame. I'm indiscriminate?" Her voice rose with the color on her cheeks.

"It takes two to tango, Jodie, and I remember both of us being involved. Look, I'm not saying you planned to get pregnant by me, but since you did, you've gone ahead and made a lot of assumptions. A lot of plans. In all fairness, I should be a part of your decisions."

"I'm not asking for much, Travis. I need your cooperation in going through the ceremony, making a few appearances, that sort of thing."

"And I need to be involved. You've had several weeks to think this through. The least you can do is give me several days."

"I'm running out of time!"

"And I'm not running to the altar again until I'm sure about who I'm marrying and why!"

JODIE FELL BACK AGAINST the bed and threw her arm over her eyes, certain she wouldn't be able to sleep even though Travis had suggested she "rest up" before dinner. Just as he'd strongly suggested she would stay with him rather than find a hotel somewhere.

She wished she could make the past five weeks go away as easily as she could shut her eyes and block out the gray Texas day. Or change just that one moment when she'd decided to step into the shower with Travis. She hadn't given a thought to protection and apparently neither had he. And now they were both paying the price.

No, she shouldn't think that. The baby was completely innocent. And Jodie realized she was already starting to have feelings for the tiny life, even though it was bad timing for a pregnancy.

In all honesty, she didn't wish she'd never met Travis. Or fallen into his bed so easily. Or anything about that weekend—but she did wish they had been more careful. A baby hadn't been part of her plans for the near future, despite the fact that she was getting to the age where she had to start seriously considering having children…or not. No, this wasn't great timing, but then, Travis certainly had good genes to give to a child. He was tall, fit, muscular and intelligent, never mind gorgeous, and had a terrific personality. Otherwise she wouldn't have fallen for him so quickly and completely.

He'd been a great guy, a fantastic lover. She'd seriously regretting leaving him on Monday to return home. He'd seemed equally sad that they'd had to part so soon.

But did he call? She shook her head. Not once. Of course, she hadn't called him, either, despite the fact he'd left her with a card. Just in case, he'd said. They'd both agreed they weren't looking for a relationship, just a brief fling. They'd known their lives weren't compatible. He was Texas; she was California. He was laid-back in his established profession; she was hard-charging about her rising career.

Apparently her egg and his sperm hadn't realized how incompatible they were outside the bedroom. The little critters had teamed up at the first chance to make a baby.

Jodie let her hand drift to her stomach. Somewhere inside a tiny life nestled, completely unconcerned about the problems of the two irresponsible adults. She couldn't let her baby down. She'd make a darn good single mother. Of course, she'd allow Travis to have visitation if he wanted to be part of the child's life. She wasn't unreasonable. On the other hand, she wouldn't push for money or anything else.

Her mother had provided a good home for her. Jodie planned to do the same for her baby. Her father hadn't wanted to be part of their family and they hadn't needed him—financially, emotionally or in any other way. Jodie had always believed that independence was the key to happiness.

A soft knock interrupted her thoughts. It took a moment for her to remember where she was—Travis's guest bedroom. Because, as he'd explained, Ranger Springs had only a two-room bed-and-breakfast, which was probably full for the weekend. She'd never been in a town without several hotels and motels—and had certainly never thought about staying in one for a couple of days while Travis digested the fact that he was going to be a father.

"Jodie?"

She swung her legs off the bed, feeling a little lightheaded when she stood. She steadied herself with a hand on the nightstand just as the door swung open.

"What's wrong?" Travis's voice showed his genuine concern and, for a moment, she wanted to once again have him hold her. She heard him stride quickly across the room, but didn't risk looking up. She didn't want to make herself any more dizzy than she already felt.

"I got up too quickly. Nothing to worry about."

"Are you sure? Have you been to the doctor yet?"

"Yes and yes. I'm sure I just need to eat a bite." She probably had been overdoing it a bit, flying from coast to coast, then stopping in Texas. Not to mention the stress of facing Travis and breaking the news so abruptly.

"Good, because I came to tell you that dinner's ready. It's not fancy, but maybe that's best on your first day here. You can get some more rest after we eat."

"I'm not that fragile, Travis," she claimed, rising to her full five-foot-eleven height. Even then, she wasn't eye level with him. She liked a big, tall man. She didn't like to think she was superficial, but she didn't date shorter, slightly built men because they made her look huge in comparison. With her height and generally "sturdy" and athletic build, she preferred a man she could look up to.

"Yes, but you are pregnant. And based on what you told me last month, I'm sure your schedule has been a little hectic lately. A few days in the Texas Hill Country is just what you need to relax."

What she needed was a husband, but she didn't say that out loud. She was certain Travis would come to the same conclusion…hopefully very soon.

"I am hungry, and I'm glad we're not going out. I've eaten every meal in a restaurant with my agent, publicist or executives for potential endorsement deals for the past five days, and I could really use a night off."

"Good. Well, I'll leave you to freshen up. Come down to the kitchen whenever you're ready."

Jodie nodded, then added, "Thanks for understanding about my schedule, Travis, but just so you're clear, I don't have days to lie around the Hill Country. I have decisions to make."

"You've already decided to have this baby, right?"

"Yes. That isn't up for discussion."

"Good, because I don't want to argue about that."

She nodded again. At least Travis wasn't the type to suggest she make this "little problem" go away.

Within a few minutes she'd splashed water on her face, brushed her hair and dabbed on a little lip gloss. There was no reason to appear glamorous when she didn't need to pose for the cameras. Besides, Travis had seen her many times over their one weekend together without makeup. Or without clothes, for that matter.

He'd just never seen her pregnant and desperate enough to ask a man she'd known for only three days to marry her.

What if he didn't say yes?

Chapter Two

"So I hear you have a very attractive lady visitor," Hank McCauley taunted on the phone line.

Travis ground his teeth and silently wished his friend a slow and painful injury.

"Not that it's any of your business," he replied, glancing toward the second-floor hallway that wrapped around the great room like a balcony. He hoped Jodie didn't walk in on him having this conversation. "She's my guest, so butt out."

"Hey, I heard she came into the Four Square Café looking for directions to your ranch. It's not my fault most of your friends and neighbors were there to gawk."

"I'll bet you were gawking most of all."

"I don't gawk at other women much since Lady Wendy and I tied the knot."

"Too bad she didn't put a zipper on your mouth."

Hank chuckled. "She likes my mouth way too much to mess with any modifications."

Travis rolled his eyes. Hank could be completely outrageous. They'd known each other since their freshman year at the University of Texas. Hank had later dropped out to pursue his rodeo career, but Travis had gone on to get his master's degree in architectural design. They'd lost touch for a few years while Hank was on the circuit. Now they were neighbors and best friends again.

Although, Travis reminded himself, with friends like that, he didn't need any enemies. The gossip mill at the café would be going full steam for several days.

For at least as long as Jodie stayed in town. Alone with him at his ranch.

"So who else were you jawin' with downtown?" He glanced at the clock over the wet bar. "It's too late for lunch."

"There was another meeting of the Fourth of July committee, which lasted longer than usual. They're getting an early start this year, planning a big parade and celebration. So yeah, basically everyone was down here and talking about you and Jodie Marsh."

"I suppose they all know by now who she is."

"Yep. Very intriguing. Of course, I had to tell them I played a role in getting you two fixed up over in Europe."

"Prince Alexi did most of the 'fixing up,' if I remember correctly." Travis, Hank and his wife, Lady Gwendolyn, and Carole and Greg Rafferty had visited Prince Alexi and Princess Kerry—a former Ranger Springs native and Carole's sister—along with the new little prince Alexander, in Belegovia in January. The country was building a new cultural center and wanted Travis to design the facility. That's where he'd been when the lot of them had arranged a blind date in Monte Carlo with Jodie, whom Alexi knew through their charitable activities.

A date that had quickly turned into a passionate weekend.

"Heck, Travis, you're the best entertainment we've got since most of us are married now. We're depending on you for a little controversy."

"Well, just leave it alone, okay? When I'm ready to tell you snoops anything, I'll give you a call."

"Tell us anything? Like what? Don't tell me the blind date got really serious. Not with Travis the Confirmed Bachelor Whitaker!"

"I'm not telling you anything. Now, if you'll excuse me, I've got a meal to prepare for a lady."

"Cooking for her, too. That does sound serious."

Travis started to hang up the phone, but Hank shouted, "Wait! Wendy wants you and Jodie to come for dinner Wednesday night. Seven o'clock, okay?"

Travis sighed. He supposed the social engagement was necessary, even if he wasn't ready to share Jodie with his friends and neighbors. "All right. See you tomorrow."

"Anyone I know?" Jodie's sexy, husky voice tore his thoughts away from his friends and neighbors and back to the woman who had just complicated his life. Not that she'd done it all alone. No, he'd participated very actively.

"Just Hank McCauley. He's as nosy as coon dog on the first day of hunting season."

"I thought he was nice."

"You just don't know him well."

"He's a good friend of yours, isn't he?"

"The jury's still out on that one," Travis replied with a shake of his head.

Jodie chuckled. "You really are a private person, aren't you?"

"I try to be. That's why I bought this ranch. I wanted to get away from the congestion and hectic pace of a big city, plus I wanted to get a few horses and run a few head of cattle. I like living in a small community, but my neighbors can be bigger gossips than the tabloids."

"Oh, I'll bet they're considerably nicer."

"That's true." Travis looked over Jodie's fresh face, glossy lips and lush figure. No one would suspect she was an internationally known model. Or that she was pregnant. She truly did appear to be "the girl next door."

"The cosmetics company made a good choice when they decided you would be their new representative."

"I beg your pardon?"

"You look so young and fresh. So ordinary, but in an extraordinary way, if that makes any sense."

"Thanks...I think."

"My thoughts were extremely complimentary even if my words didn't convey my feelings."

She turned away, looking a bit embarrassed. "In that case, thanks again."

"Are you hungry?"

"Famished. How may I help?"

"Why don't you get some glasses out of that cabinet," he said, gesturing with the salad tongs, "and decide what you'd like to drink."

He turned his attention back to the roasted chicken

he'd fixed in his smoker last night. It was his favorite meal, although he never let on to his cattle-ranching friends that he preferred chicken over a nice big steak. Folks had been run out of Texas for less.

When he turned to get the potato salad out of the refrigerator, he and Jodie collided. With a gasp, she stepped back.

"Sorry," he said. "I'm not used to having someone else in the kitchen."

"My fault," she said breathlessly, looking flushed and adorable. "I'm not used to being in someone else's kitchen."

He did his best to ignore the feeling of Jodie's breasts brushing against his arm, but like the proverbial elephant in the room, he could barely think of anything else. Despite the distraction, though, within a few minutes they had the meal on the table.

"So," he said after they'd started their salads, "tell me again why I should break every promise I made to myself about getting married again."

"I'VE ALREADY EXPLAINED about the contract, the morality clause and my career. I don't see how it could be any more clear."

"What about how you feel about having this baby? How you'd feel about getting married? I don't think either one was in your plans for the near future."

"No, they weren't, but the pregnancy happened. I can't change that." Some women might, and that was fine for them, but eliminating "the problem" wasn't something she could do. Not when she had other options. She was going to have this baby, even if it meant giving up the contract—which she wasn't about to admit to Travis. Her mother and her agent had always told her to negotiate from a point of strength. Never admit your weaknesses. Compromise, but don't settle.

"I'm glad to hear it. Now, you've told me all the logical reasons why you need to get married. Tell me how you're feeling about it."

Wow, this was a reversal. A man asking her to talk about her feelings? Had she entered an alternate universe when she'd driven across the Ranger Springs city limit? "I feel like I should do the right thing. I feel like I want this baby to have a mother who can provide for him or her."

"That's just more logic. What about getting married? How are you going to react to us living together as man and wife? Are you ready to compromise, or have you even considered me in your plans?"

"I...of course I've considered you." She wouldn't have considered marrying someone she couldn't tolerate. But then, she wouldn't have gotten pregnant by a man who was repulsive. "I didn't think marriage—especially a temporary marriage—to me would be that distasteful."

"I've been married before and I made a vow that I never would again. I don't make vows lightly, Jodie. There's a reason I'm against the institution of marriage."

"Why? What happened to make you bitter?"

"Who said I'm bitter? There are other reasons to want to avoid the state of matrimony."

She couldn't think of any. "So, what happened between you two?"

"I don't talk about that time in my life."

"Oh, but it's fine to grill me about my life?"

"Ask me whatever you want to know about my life right now and I'll answer the questions. But I didn't ask you about your past and I don't want to discuss mine."

"Just tell me this. Is there anything in your past that would damage my career if we were to marry and the information was leaked to the media?"

He thought for a moment. Took another bite of salad, chewed and swallowed. "No."

She breathed a sigh of relief. "Okay then. What's the problem? We liked each other well enough five weeks ago. I'm not that difficult to live with. As I mentioned, I won't even be around all that much. Why, you'd hardly know I was here."

"And this is supposed to make me feel better…why?"

"Because I'm not asking much from you in the way of compromise! I'm trying to be thoughtful."

He pushed his half-eaten salad aside. "I'd like to be thoughtful *before* we stand in front of a minister."

"A justice of the peace or even an Elvis impersonator at a wedding chapel would be fine with me, as long as the marriage is legal."

"I'm not running away to Las Vegas or going to some county clerk's office to get married."

"Fine. Then we'll do whatever you'd like. After all, you're doing me—and the baby, of course—a favor by agreeing to marry me."

"Okay, then answer this. What's in it for me?"

Jodie immediately thought of twisted sheets and hot, damp bodies. Not that they'd talked about having a sex life *after* the ceremony. Pushing the image aside, she sighed. "The knowledge that you're doing the right thing?"

"Maybe you don't know me very well. Maybe I'm not the kind of guy who wants to do the right thing. Maybe I'm irresponsible and selfish."

She didn't think for a minute that was the case. Travis had been a generous and inventive lover—not the kind of man who thought only of himself. "I'm not buying that line. I think you're a man who would acknowledge his child, who would try to help that child's mother out of a difficult situation."

"And you're basing this on…?"

"Just what I know about you! You're a nice guy, Travis Whitaker. I wouldn't have gone to bed with you on our first date if you hadn't been." She pushed aside her salad bowl, surprised to note she'd eaten most of the healthy green stuff without ever thinking about it.

He looked amused as he calmly cut into his roasted chicken. "Okay, maybe I'm a fairly nice guy. At least most of the time. When I'm not dealing with a temperamental client or an incompetent contractor. Or a stubborn cow or a nosy friend. But that doesn't mean I'm good marriage material. You can't be sure I'd be a good father."

"I think you'd try. And besides, if you don't want to be a part of this baby's life, you don't have to be. I'm not trying to force you to take part in parenting if that's not what you want. I have the money to hire a nanny, to pay for the best schools and to give this child a wonderful future. I'd like for you to be a part of his or her life, but it's not necessary."

"It's necessary to me."

"Then what's the problem?" She felt like throwing up her hands in exasperation. They kept having circular arguments, with Travis revealing as little as possible about how he felt, but asking her to bare her soul.

"The problem is that you marched in here demanding that we get married on your terms. You didn't even let me be happy about seeing you again before you were telling me your plans and expecting me to play this minimalist role of husband and father." He pushed his plate aside and leaned closer. "Well, Jodie Marsh, maybe that's not what I want. Did you ever think of that? Did you ever consider that I might have other plans?"

She sat back in her chair, feeling as if the floor had shifted beneath her. When they'd first met, she hadn't considered Travis's life much at all. She'd never asked him personal details, such as if he had someone back in Texas. Because he'd been so hot for her, she'd assumed he was unattached. "Oh, God. Do you already have a fiancée? A serious girlfriend?"

Travis laughed. "Relax and finish your dinner, Jodie. You're eating for two now."

"That's an old wives' tale. And you didn't answer my question." Still, she took a bite of tender chicken and followed it with some potato salad.

"No, I don't have a fiancée or a serious girlfriend. What would be the point of getting engaged? I already told you I'd never planned to marry."

"Then you never wanted children?"

A look of pain, maybe regret, passed over his face, but it was gone before she could wonder too much about his past. The one he didn't want to discuss.

"I have friends with children. I have a sister who has a son. If I feel the urge to be around the little monsters, I have opportunities."

"You think all children are monsters?" she asked.

"No, I was just joking. I'm actually quite good around them. I can even change diapers."

"You have me beat, then, because I don't have the foggiest idea how to care for a baby." She took another forkful of food while she waited for him to chide her for being unprepared. "Although I do like children."

"No brothers or sisters? No nieces or nephews?"

Once again he'd surprised her by not rubbing her nose in her inadequacies. "I have a younger sister, Chelsea, who is twenty-seven. My mother divorced when I was three and never remarried."

Travis nodded. "I have nothing against children, but since I'd never planned to marry, I didn't think the opportunity would arise. Also, I like my freedom. I take jobs I want, I travel quite often and I have my ranch to keep me from being bored. I don't think I'd make a good candidate for a single dad, in the unlikely event I decided to adopt. Which I've never seriously considered."

"Sometimes nature takes over and we become better parents than we could have imagined."

"I've heard that. I've also seen parents who tried awfully hard and were terrible at the job."

"I'm not going to be terrible. I'm going to be a terrific mom. I'm going to ask my mother how she raised such a great kid—namely, me—and then follow her example."

Travis laughed. "All that and modest, too."

"Darn right."

She looked down at her plate and saw that she'd eaten all of her chicken and potato salad, along with a handful of grapes. She and Travis had been talking so intently that she'd been oblivious.

"Did you have time to unpack?" he asked as he reached for her plate.

"I don't mind living out of my suitcase. I'm used to it."

"Jodie, why don't you unpack? You're going to be here awhile."

"I am?"

"Well, aren't you going to try to talk me into getting married? Or have you changed your mind?"

She shook her head. "No. But like I mentioned, I'm on a really tight schedule. I'm counting down nine months!"

"Giving me a week or so isn't going to make any difference."

"It might!"

"Jodie, given the fact that we're both tall and not skinny, I don't think this baby is going to be a tiny little thing. We're not going to pass it off as premature."

"Well..."

"Just unpack, relax and enjoy a short vacation in Ranger Springs. Get to know the people. Get to know me."

"So I'm supposed to relax while you make the most important decision of my life?"

"That's right."

"How about you go ahead and decide, then we can both relax?"

"I'm going to defy my basic nature and not rush into this decision."

"You were willing to rush into my hotel suite in Monte Carlo!" she exclaimed, putting her hands on her hips and glaring at him. Probably not the smartest move when she was still trying to get his compliance, but she could only take so much baiting.

"That was...different."

"Make an exception!"

"About getting married? I can't do that, no matter how much I like and respect you."

"You...you like me?"

"Of course I like you. Do you think I sleep with women I can't stand?"

"No, but—"

"Even though I like you, I can't just jump into marriage. I have to think this through."

"What do you want, legal agreements? No problem. I'll have my lawyers draw up a prenuptial. I'll make whatever promises you need if you'll just cooperate."

"Give me some time, Jodie. I want to do what's best for all of us."

"I know what's best! I've already explained what we need to do and why."

"No, Jodie. You know what's best for your career. I'm talking about our lives and the life of our baby."

AFTER THE MEAL, Travis excused himself, saying he had some chores. In truth, he just needed to get away. Away from Jodie's tempting presence. Away from his chaotic thoughts. Since she'd arrived back in his life a few hours ago, she'd turned his thinking completely around. His future now included a child—and possibly a wife.

But for how long? Jodie said she expected their marriage to be "temporary." He didn't like the sound of that. In his opinion, temporary items tended to be inferior in quality and comfort.

He liked to build things to last.

Fortunately the showers had stopped shortly after Jodie arrived. The ground was soft, the dry winter grass slick with rain, but not enough to keep him indoors. He saddled one of the horses he'd purchased from Hank several months ago, glad he had the acres and the time to ride. There was something about being in the saddle that cleared his head, centering him in this suddenly mixed-up world.

His favorite spot was only a fifteen-minute ride away, just over a small hill and around a stand of pecan and live oak trees he hadn't yet thinned. He'd have to do that later in the year for firewood. Using a chain saw and a hatchet was right up there with chest thumping for manly pursuits.

At the base of the hill was a small swimming hole formed by the springs for which the town was named back in the 1880s when a Texas Ranger was shot by outlaws. According to local lore, a widow living nearby had nursed him back to health using water from the spring.

Travis wasn't sure whether the story was true or not, but the spring was a refreshing relief from the summer heat. On this cool, late winter day, he wouldn't be swimming, but he still liked to visit the spot where the water bubbled up from the underground aquifer and ran out into the stream that bisected the town.

Usually the peaceful spot helped him relax. But today, as the sun set and the sky turned to deep pink and mauve, he knew he didn't have answers. Should he marry Jodie—even temporarily? The idea didn't set well with him. He and Jodie needed to find a compromise, but all she wanted was a temporary husband to satisfy her contract.

He didn't want to be anyone's disposable husband. But did he want to be a permanent part of Jodie's life when he'd sworn he'd never marry again?

Chapter Three

Jodie spent some time soaking in the big bathtub in Travis's guest suite, wondering where he'd gone so suddenly after the early dinner he'd served her. It had been dark for several hours and he hadn't returned. Should she go looking for him? Call someone? Where would she report a missing rancher? Dialing 9-1-1 seemed extreme when the man in question was probably just avoiding further discussion of their situation.

She sighed and decided the water was too cool to stay in any longer. She rose from the tub, then went through her nightly ritual of brisk towel-drying and moisturizing. Her skin was one of her best features. She took very good care of her assets.

After dressing for bed in a short gown and longer robe, she wandered into the bedroom. She wasn't used to having so much free time. She should have picked up a new novel to read, but she hadn't been thinking clearly. She'd just impulsively booked a flight to Texas to talk to Travis.

The father of her baby.

"Could you want to be a daddy, Travis?" she murmured as she looked out the window. There were lights in the barn, but she didn't know if they were automatic or if it meant someone was working in there. If *Travis* was there, avoiding her.

The house was so quiet that she turned on the small CD player she found in the entertainment cabinet. After searching through several country-western stations, she located one that played some generic sort of easy listening. Curled up in a chair where she could see the barn, she let the tension drain out of her as the music flowed in. She shouldn't be sleepy, but she was, perhaps because of the time zone change, perhaps because of the pregnancy.

Outside the window, a branch from a tree swayed in the night wind. She felt the hypnotic pull, aware that she was drifting off, but not caring at the moment. She was safe and warm, she'd presented her plan to Travis, and all she could do was wait for him to agree.

TRAVIS REMOVED HIS BOOTS in the mudroom, walked quietly over the cold slate floors, then toward the master bedroom. Before he went looking for Jodie, he needed a shower and a change of clothes.

He hadn't found solace at his favorite spot, but he had been able to think while he'd cleaned out stalls. His barn now sported the cleanest floors, the most spotless feed buckets and the neatest tack room in the entire Hill Country.

And he'd come to some conclusions. He needed to

throw out his vow to never marry again. Jodie had presented him with the one reason that would get him back to the altar—a child. He wouldn't have married for companionship or sex or any other reason since he could have all those things without the problems a wife represented. His past experience had made him associate marriage with manipulation, frustration and disappointment. But that was marriage based on love—or more accurately, two people who thought they were in love. He and Jodie didn't suffer from that delusion. If they married, it would be for sound, logical reasons.

He stripped quickly and eased beneath the warm water, grateful that he'd installed a top-of-the-line shower stall with multiple jets of water to soothe tired muscles. Big enough for two. Not that he expected Jodie to open the glass door and join him, but that was exactly how their baby had been conceived.

Thinking back, he even knew the date. January fourth. He counted forward nine months. That meant their child would be born around October first. By Halloween, he could get one of those cute costumes for the baby. By Christmas, he'd have a son or daughter to buy gifts for. The idea was mind-boggling, nearly surreal, since Jodie looked exactly the same as she had when they'd first met.

He certainly hadn't planned on having children— since he'd sworn never to marry again—but now it was almost all he could think about. Unlike his own father, he wanted to be a dad who changed diapers and took his child to the mall and read stories to him at night.

Would Jodie try to exclude him from their baby's life, just as she'd tried to make all the decisions about their relationship? Their marriage?

He showered quickly, dried off and dressed in comfortable sweats. The house was silent as he made his way down the hall. The few lights on automatic timers revealed no sign of his guest. She hadn't been in the kitchen, or if she had, she was one neat person. Not a glass or spoon was out of place.

He silently climbed the steps. Walking softly in his socks, he paused outside the guest bedroom. The faint sound of music filtered through the thick oak door. He knocked softly.

She might be sleeping. He'd heard that pregnant women needed lots of naps and a good night's sleep. If so, he didn't want to bother her. But the urge to check on Jodie, to make sure she was comfortable, overwhelmed his need to respect her privacy—and his good sense. He slowly turned the knob and eased open the door.

By the soft glow of an accent lamp, he saw her curled up in a chair beside the window. Her feet rested on an ottoman and she'd hugged her arms around herself, tugging her robe tight. She should be wrapped in a soft throw or blanket, but she hadn't taken the time to do so before she'd fallen asleep.

He leaned down and looked out the window. She'd been watching the barn, he realized. Was she worried about him? Had she thought he'd gone off and deserted her?

He should have been more forthcoming about where

he was going and how long he would be gone. He should have been more thoughtful, but he wasn't used to having someone around. He'd had a few guests beside his sister Kate and her family, but no one else had ever lived in this house. He'd designed and built it after his divorce, when he'd moved to Ranger Springs to escape life in the city.

There was usually no one around to wonder what he was doing in the barn or to worry about him working through meals in his studio or to care whether he stayed out late at Schultze's Roadhouse. And he liked it that way, he reminded himself.

He pulled a soft throw from the bench at the foot of the bed and draped it over Jodie. She stirred but didn't awaken. He tucked the ends around her feet and she opened her eyes.

"Travis," she sighed. Her husky, sexy voice invaded his mind and body like a mild electric current, putting him on alert. This was no time for sexual desire or any feelings that would sidetrack him. His focus would stay on what he had to say, because he had to make Jodie understand his position.

"You must be tired," he said.

"I'm blaming it mostly on the time zone changes."

"I'm thinking it has something to do with the baby."

"Could be," she murmured as she stretched. "Other than being a little more tired than usual, I haven't noticed any changes."

"No morning sickness?"

"No. I've been lucky."

"I'm glad. That doesn't sound like fun. I remember listening to my sister Kate and Kerry Jacks talk about their pregnancies. I thought then that pregnancy would be really tough on women who worked outside the home."

"I sure wouldn't want to have a lot of assignments, especially if I had to fly, if I were sick every morning."

"You'll be cutting back on your assignments now, right?"

"Very soon. Even though I'm plus size, a round tummy is going to show. I'll probably stick with chest-high shots and my cosmetics obligations through the pregnancy."

"But you won't be working all the time, will you?"

"No, of course not."

"Because I want you to take care of yourself and the baby. I don't want you to overdo it."

"I won't." She frowned. "But why the concern? I'm healthy. I'm not expecting any complications."

"Can't I be concerned? I care about you. And this is my baby, too, right?"

"Right." She paused, then shifted in the chair, bringing his attention to her full breasts.

"So…where were you tonight?"

He looked back into her eyes. "Just doing some chores." She didn't have to know that he had a helper who cleaned the stalls and maintained the tack for him when he was busy with a project or out of town. "Thinking, too."

"Oh? About what?"

"Us. The baby. What you want to do about it."

She shifted in the chair, sitting up straighter. "Did you come to any conclusions?"

He could tell that what she really wanted to ask was, "Have you decided to do things on my terms?"

"Yes, I did." He reached for her hands, noting they were cool and dry. He felt tiny tremors pass through her body, as though she was trembling in anticipation. "First, I have to ask you something."

"What?"

"Do you think what we felt in Monte Carlo was real?"

"What do you mean, real? I certainly wasn't faking anything!"

"I mean, do you think the immediate attraction we felt was genuine? Or was it a fluke? When you look back on that time, do you say to yourself that you were stupid? Or do you remember the weekend fondly?"

"Well…I think we were irresponsible that one time, but overall, I don't think anything that happened was stupid. I don't think we reacted to each other any differently there than if we'd been introduced in New York or L.A. And despite the inconvenient timing of this pregnancy, I can't say that I'm sorry that we made a baby together."

"For the record, I'm happy about the baby, too. It took me a while to get used to the idea, since I hadn't planned to get married or to have children."

"Well, it hasn't been so long. I just showed up on your doorstep right after lunch."

"True, but I'm an intuitive kind of guy. I just needed some time to think about us in relation to this…new development."

"Still, this was a pretty big shock, I think."

"I'm glad you told me right away, though."

"It was only fair, especially since I also asked you to marry me right away."

"Speaking of marriage, I've been giving it a lot of thought."

"And?"

"I understand your position about your career and the contract you signed."

"I feel a big 'but' coming on," she said, pulling her hands away from his and tugging her robe tighter.

"I also believe that having two parents is best for a child."

"Best, perhaps, but not necessary."

"The thing is," he continued, deciding to ignore her comments for the moment. She could get him into a tangential conversation far too easily. "I've been giving your ideas on marriage a lot of thought. And I simply don't agree with your premise."

"Which premise is that?"

"That this needs to be temporary. That we have no basis upon which to build a deeper relationship."

"You want to stay married longer? For the sake of the baby?"

"If we get married, I want to stay married *period*. That's how marriage is supposed to work."

"But often doesn't."

"True. I'm a perfect example of how it's sometimes necessary to end a marriage." Getting a divorce was the best thing possible, given his ex-wife Tiffany's priorities. He wasn't about to be labeled a two-time loser, especially not now that he'd set down roots in a place he loved. If he married then divorced Jodie, people who cared about him would be understanding, but they'd still know he'd failed twice—either by choosing the wrong women to marry or by being unable to compromise and care enough to hold them.

"This time, I'm older and wiser. If I stand before a minister or an official of the state and say my vows, I need to mean them." He looked deeply into Jodie's troubled eyes. "I need to know you mean them, too."

"Travis, you're making a bigger issue out of this than it needs to be. There's no reason to make this into a big production with lifetime consequences."

He pulled back, his anger rising until he told himself that Jodie was scared. He could see it in her eyes. She felt as if she might lose the career she'd built based on her image. She was pregnant and single. And she didn't want a lifetime commitment from him because she didn't believe in the feelings they'd shared for one weekend in Monte Carlo.

Not that he believed in love. Depending on that fleeting emotion would be like building a house on shifting sand. Anyone could say they loved you, swear that they'd love you forever, without it meaning anything. The attraction, the mutual respect, the companionship he and Jodie shared—those were real.

He was convinced they could get those feelings back. He knew it when he looked at her sleeping in his guest room or in unguarded moments when she allowed her vulnerability to peek through the polished veneer she showed the rest of the world.

"Like it or not, we've made a lifetime commitment by creating a child together."

"We can have a responsibility to the child without having one to each other."

"Maybe you can. I don't think so, but I might be wrong. But I can't function that way. We should have a commitment to stay married or we don't get married at all."

"You're giving me an ultimatum?"

"Just like you handed me one when you walked in the door."

"That was different. I was trying to be considerate. I never wanted you to think that I was trying to trap you into marriage. You must know I didn't plan to get pregnant. That's why I still believe a temporary marriage would be best."

"Jodie, I'm absolutely serious when I tell you this. We're getting married on Saturday, which is Valentine's Day, at Bretford House in Ranger Springs. That's where we normally have receptions for local weddings. I would suggest having the ceremony in the church, but they're refinishing the floors right now."

He paused to take a breath. "It takes three days in Texas to get a license and make the arrangements. The date will seem romantic when your publicist prepares a press release about our whirlwind courtship."

"Three days to plan a wedding!"

"You'll have one day to decide, then we need to go to the county clerk's office to apply for a license. I suggest you call your relatives, friends and business associates tomorrow and make travel arrangements for them. I'll take care of the rest."

She looked completely stunned as she sat upright in the chair, framed by the window. In the dark glass he saw a reflection of the room. He saw himself, looking stiff and determined. Well, fine. That's how he felt. His decision was firm—he wasn't getting married again unless it was for keeps. Maybe he and Jodie didn't have enough in common to build a marriage, but maybe, just maybe, they did.

At least this time his wife wouldn't beseech him to tell her he loved her one more time. To prove that he loved her by giving in to her demands for more, more, more. Jodie wasn't insecure and clingy; she wouldn't need constant reassurance.

He turned away from his austere image, then remembered an earlier conversation. "Oh, and by the way, we're having dinner Wednesday night with Hank and Gwendolyn McCauley. Seven o'clock."

"Travis, you can't just come in here and turn my world upside down like this!"

"Funny you should say that, sweetheart, because that's exactly what you did to me earlier today."

She ignored his sarcasm. "I need time. I need to consult with my attorney and agent. I have plans to make!"

"Jodie, if you want to get married to me, you'd better

make those plans in a hurry, because come Saturday, there's going to be a wedding. It's not going to be the biggest or the most elaborate wedding ever, but it's going to be public, it's going to be legal and it's going to be ours."

Chapter Four

Jodie had slept little after Travis's dramatic announcement last night. She'd barely dozed off when her travel alarm buzzed. Now, showered and dressed, she felt ill prepared for what today would bring.

Still, she walked with as much confidence as she could muster down the second-floor hallway, pausing to look at the great room below. There was no fire in the large hearth, but she smelled coffee and sensed warmth coming from the kitchen. Apparently, Travis was already up, or he had a housekeeper. To take care of this large residence, Jodie wouldn't be surprised if he had live-in help—not that she'd seen anyone yesterday.

She and Travis needed to talk about his ultimatum and she'd much rather do that in private, without even a one-person audience. She still thought a temporary marriage was best. Certainly they needed a whole new plan if he insisted they stay married. Not that she believed they would, of course. They had separate lives and might find that they weren't compatible if they spent months rather than days together. The one thing they had in common was the baby, and she was willing to share the child with Travis. Surely they could be civilized and compromise on custody.

She hadn't spent too much time thinking about marriage—although like many women, she'd fantasized about the perfect wedding. She'd been too busy rising in her profession. She'd always assumed one day she'd fall in love, get married and have children. In that order. Now she was doing it in reverse, only there was no guarantee of "falling in love." But how could she get what she needed—a cooperative husband—without giving up on her dreams?

She couldn't even call her mother, sister or publicist in California yet. They wouldn't appreciate being awakened at six o'clock in the morning, West Coast time. But as soon as she and Travis talked again and came to a realistic agreement on their marriage, she'd let her people, family and friends know.

Perhaps a small private ceremony with a minister or justice of the peace wouldn't be too bad. But Valentine's Day? That was certainly quick, which was one of her needs, but was it too quick? When she'd told him they needed to get married right away, she was thinking of flying off to Vegas or Reno. Having a quiet ceremony. Perhaps with one photo that could be released to the press.

She had the perfect dress in her closet in Newport Beach. A creamy silk organza with embroidery that she'd purchased in India last year. The dress was beautiful, but she hadn't found the perfect place to wear it…yet. She'd add medium-height Ferragamo's and some polished capiz shell and pearl jewelry from her favorite Los Angeles designer. She'd look romantic yet sophisticated, especially on the arm of such a handsome, tall man dressed in black, classic Ralph Lauren.

She stopped and frowned. Surely she wasn't shallow enough to consider the father of her child as an accessory! No, that's not how she felt, she realized. She was just so accustomed to thinking in terms of how she looked in public that when she'd included him in the mental picture, she'd made him seem like part of her ensemble.

But Travis was much more. He was opinionated and decisive. Sexy and smart, yet perfectly at home in all types of situations. He possessed a strong sense of values that she admired, even when they conflicted with her need to do what was right for her life, her career and their baby.

A movement below caught her eye. As though she'd conjured him up by thinking so hard about him, he appeared. Wearing a sea-green crew-necked cotton sweater, faded jeans and heavy-soled boots, he looked every inch the wealthy, country gentleman. He could be a model for a new Chaps ad campaign.

"Didn't anyone tell you that frowning causes wrinkles?" he said in a faintly teasing tone, placing his hands on his hips and staring up at her.

She smoothed away her expression, surprised she'd let him see her emotions so clearly. "Obviously, I'm not using Botox," she quipped, thinking of all her acquaintances who had the injections to paralyze the muscles that caused frown lines on their foreheads.

"What's troubling you?"

You, she felt like shouting. But that wouldn't accomplish anything, especially when she needed his cooperation. "I have a few things on my mind."

"Join the crowd," he said with a sigh. "Come down and have some breakfast. Then I'll help you with any plans you need to make."

She turned away toward the spiral staircase leading to the first floor, feeling the telltale frown return. Her hand gripped the metal banister until her newly polished nails threatened to snap. She didn't need his help planning— she needed his agreement that they would cooperate on a temporary marriage, she thought as she tromped down the steps. She needed him to make the media believe they'd fallen madly in love in Monte Carlo and were getting married because they couldn't bear to be apart.

Well, at least not too far apart for too long, since she planned to continue her scheduled assignments and he probably had commissions to design buildings. Once the news of their hurried, hushed wedding hit the press and they'd granted a few choice interviews, she and Travis could go back to leading their separate lives most of the time. Then she'd fly back to Texas as often as possible and he could visit her in California, especially when she had a function to attend.

Especially when she started showing her pregnancy. She'd need a supportive husband then.

She walked into the breakfast area of the spacious kitchen. She smelled bacon and commented, "You're quite the cook."

"Not really. I just know enough to get by. I have a housekeeper, Helen Kaminsky, who comes twice a week. She'll be here tomorrow and you can meet her. If I'm in town and on a project, she sometimes prepares meals for me. Otherwise, I go shopping myself. I'm amazed by the new prepared food at the grocery stores."

She couldn't picture Travis Whitaker pushing a cart through a supermarket, although she had no problem thinking of him in formal attire or country casual or cowboy chic. The fact that they knew so little about each other's lives accentuated the need to avoid a permanent commitment. They'd have plenty of time to get to know each other well enough to mutually support a child, however, if Travis decided to stay involved.

"I'm constantly amazed at the variety of food available in restaurants," she replied, forcing her attention back to breakfast.

"Maybe in New York or L.A., but you'll find the choices much more limited in Ranger Springs."

"But surely you have restaurants."

"A few. The Four Square Café for breakfast and lunch. A pizza place that delivers. That's a fairly recent addition. There's a Tex-Mex place on the state highway, a fast-food burger chain and then there's Bretford House for lunch or dinner. That's where we'll be having the wedding."

"If we can agree on terms."

He turned toward a beep from the oven. As he pulled a pan of perfectly browned biscuits out, he said, "There's really not much to talk about. I'll be glad to sign a prenuptial agreement if you'd like. We can each agree to keep whatever we came with into the marriage, although that's pretty much the law in Texas anyway. Since there's no baby yet, we don't need to address that issue right now. Other than inviting family, I'm not sure what else is necessary."

"How can you be so calm, so glib, about this? Surely you don't get married every day!" At his chuckle she added, "Do you? You mentioned one ex-wife, but are there more?"

Travis shook his head, making a lock of tawny hair fall over his forehead. "No, one was quite enough, which is a really good reason not to have another one. *Ex*-wife, that is," he clarified as he dumped the biscuits into a basket and covered them with a napkin.

"What was she like?" Jodie asked before she could stop herself. His past relationships weren't really her business, but she was curious about his ex. In Monte Carlo he'd been so adamant that he wasn't looking for anything past a great weekend. Had his marriage been a disaster? Her fault...or his?

He shrugged, carrying the biscuits and butter to the table. "Tiffany was cute and clever. Petite. Dainty, I suppose, but only in appearance. Inside she was a ten-foot-long great white shark with a huge appetite for anything that caught her eye."

"And I'm sure you caught her eye," Jodie commented, grabbing the plate of bacon and carrying it to the table. He'd set two places with place mats and heavy, dark blue ceramic plates.

"If you're thinking of love at first sight, you're wrong. She decided I was moving up and could give her what she wanted." He pulled out two chairs and indicated where Jodie should sit.

She smiled to herself when she noticed the tall glass of milk at her place setting. "Which was?"

He settled into his seat before answering. "Everything. I never understood what Tiffany really wanted, but she was sure glad to look under every label and price tag to find it."

"Other than spending your money, what was the problem?"

He placed his fork and knife down with a clatter. "Look, let's not talk about her anymore, okay? It's over and done with. I was young and stupid when we married, older and wiser when we got divorced. It doesn't have anything to do with this marriage."

Jodie didn't want to argue with him, but she thought that anything from their past might affect their marriage—even if it were temporary. Nevertheless, she could understand why he didn't want to discuss his ex-wife with his possible future wife, so she kept silent. There would be time to talk later—if they actually got married.

"I'd like to see the town if you have time this morning. And this Bretford House where we're going to have the ceremony, if we get married."

"On Valentine's Day," he added. "Four days from now."

Jodie sighed. The man had a one-track mind. "So, do you have time or not?"

He nodded while chewing a bite of biscuit. After swallowing, he added, "I haven't started on my next project yet because I'm waiting on some additional site elevations from the surveyor. I can put that off until after the wedding."

"Great." All this seemed to be falling into place for him, while she still felt completely turned around. She couldn't remember her schedule. Thankfully, it was all written down in her trusty planner. She knew she had to be back in California next week, but wasn't sure what date.

If she didn't value her independence so much, she'd hire a personal assistant to travel with her. But she didn't want someone with her all the time. How would she get used to a husband if they actually lived together?

She couldn't. She'd just have to explain that to Travis after they went through with the ceremony he wanted. Something for him. Something for her. Isn't that what compromise was all about?

TRAVIS TRIED TO SEE his adopted hometown through Jodie's much more sophisticated eyes, but he had a hard time reading her expressions as he parked his SUV in front of Schuler's Jewelry Store. If looking around and meeting folks went well, he hoped they could shop for wedding bands before going to Bretford House to finalize the wedding plans.

The town square appeared rather bleak on this February day, with only a few evergreen shrubs to break the faded browns of this past winter. Soon spring bulbs would appear, but today he suspected Jodie wouldn't see the charm of the gazebo or walkways used by so many in Ranger Springs.

"The town square is real nice in the spring and summer," Travis commented as they stepped onto the sidewalk.

Jodie nodded, but was obviously busy looking around. "The businesses seem to be doing well," she finally said.

"We're having a small boom. More and more people are moving out of the cities and into the countryside."

"It's…charming."

Not exactly wild praise, but he'd settle for her favorable impression. "The café is on the other side of the square, near the gazebo. I thought we'd go there first and meet some of the regulars."

He and Jodie walked side by side. He felt as though he should hold her hand, or take her arm, or make some other gesture, but he couldn't read her mood. She wasn't exactly as chilly as the wind whipping along the raised concrete sidewalk, but she didn't seem all warm and snuggly, either.

Despite her somewhat subdued mood, he enjoyed walking with a woman he didn't have to lean down to talk to, or saunter beside slowly because their strides were so different. The kind of women he usually dated wore heels almost everywhere, and they giggled when he commented on how "little" they were. Jodie didn't giggle, although in the days they'd spent together, she'd laughed and chuckled regularly. She had a throaty, genuine laugh that came from deep inside. He hadn't realized how irritating a high-pitched, childish voice could be on a grown woman until he'd met Jodie.

The door to the Four Square Café tinkled in welcome as he stepped inside. Normally he took a table near the front window, but he didn't want to appear antisocial by ignoring the folks who were lingering over their coffee. None of the waitresses were up front, so he grabbed a couple of menus before guiding Jodie past the old-fashioned chrome and Formica-topped tables to the rear booths.

"Mornin', Ambrose. You're looking pretty today, Joyce," he greeted the semiretired doctor and his new wife. "Dr. and Mrs. Wheatley, I'd like you to meet Jodie Marsh. She's going to be in town for a few days until she needs to go back to Los Angeles."

"Why, hello there, dear. You're the famous model, aren't you?" Joyce asked. "Thelma told me she'd met you yesterday. You just missed her, by the way."

Jodie chuckled. "I don't know how famous I am, Mrs. Wheatley, but I do model. I'm not sure I remember who Thelma is, though."

"Thelma Rogers. She's the owner, editor and lead reporter for the *Springs Gazette*, our local newspaper."

"Oh, really?"

Travis sensed Jodie's concern over hearing that the newspaper editor already knew she was in town. "The *Gazette* is a weekly paper, and besides, Thelma doesn't run any tabloid-style stories."

"Oh, I'm sure she doesn't. I was just hoping to have a nice, quiet stay here for a few days."

"I'll bet you go to lots of exciting places for your work," Joyce said.

"I stay fairly busy, but I don't work all the time. There's a growing market for plus-size clothes for business, casual and exercise wear. And I have some other… things I'm working on right now, too."

Travis wondered if she meant her cosmetics contract or their baby.

"You're not one of those skinny little beanpoles, either," Dr. Wheatley added. "They look downright anemic to me." He shuddered. "I like a woman with a good figure, like my sweetie here," he added, patting Joyce's hand.

The strawberry-blond hairdresser smiled and practically blushed. *Newlyweds,* Travis thought with a mental shake of his head. Ambrose and Joyce were just two more of the happily married couples populating Ranger Springs. Two more of the people making goo-goo eyes at each other and acting as silly as teenagers. Getting married without all that silliness made a lot more sense to him.

Jodie smiled at the older couple. "No one's ever confused me for a beanpole. I tried dieting when I was a teenager, but I soon discovered that I couldn't keep my weight down to a size six. It's much more fun to eat enough to keep my weight up to a size sixteen."

"Just as long as you exercise and eat right," the doctor added.

"Believe me, I do."

"Well, it's so nice to meet you, Jodie. I hope you have a nice visit in our town. It's a good place to…well, settle down if you wanted to live somewhere normal."

The Ranger Springs matchmakers were still alive and well, Travis thought with fondness. Joyce and her sidekick, Thelma Rogers, had participated in several matchmaking projects over the past few years with great success. If one measured success by marriages, that is.

Jodie laughed. "I'll remember that."

Travis took her elbow. "I'd like to introduce you to Charlene Jacks, Kerry's mother. She still works here at the café, although most of us assumed she'd retire now that two of her daughters are married to very successful men. Carole's husband is CEO of a large food company."

"I'd love to meet her. Although I knew Alexi first, I've really enjoyed getting to know Kerry, also. And their son Alexander is adorable."

The little boy was cute. Which reminded Travis that this time next year, he'd have a little boy or girl who would be equally adorable. Their baby would no doubt have blond hair, since he knew for a fact that Jodie was a natural blonde. And when the child grew up, he or she would be tall. If they had a son, he'd probably be muscular and athletic. A daughter would no doubt be long-limbed and curvy.

He'd have to lock her up until she was thirty, just in case she had any interest in boys.

"Travis?"

He shook himself out of his daydreaming and smiled at Jodie. "Sorry. I was just about to take you back to meet Charlene."

They walked to the rear of the restaurant, toward the booths near the pickup window. The smell of bacon still hung in the air, but soon the fryer would be producing chicken-fried steak and French fries, and the grill would be full of burgers.

"Mornin', Charlene," he said to the woman rolling flatware inside white paper napkins.

"Travis! Good to see you."

He leaned down and kissed her cheek. "That's from Alexi." Travis had talked to him just two days ago to discuss plans for the cultural center he was designing.

"I've been blessed with two wonderful sons-in-law." She chuckled, a gleam in her blue eyes. "Now all I need is one more for Cheryl and all my girls will be happily married."

"Don't look at me!" Travis replied, feigning horror.

Charlene laughed, then smiled at Jodie. "And who is this lovely lady?"

"Charlene Jacks, allow me to introduce Jodie Marsh. I'm sure you've already heard she's in town."

"Yes, indeed. Welcome to Ranger Springs, Ms. Marsh."

"Please, call me Jodie. And I'm very glad to be here, and to meet you. I've known Alexi for several years and I've really enjoyed getting to know Kerry. She's a delightful addition to the royal family."

"I like to think so. And what about that baby of theirs? Isn't he the most adorable child ever?"

Jodie chuckled. "He's a cutie."

She glanced at Travis and he could almost hear her thoughts. *Our child will be cute, too.* He smiled in reply.

"Would you like a table or a booth? It's a bit early for lunch, but I could get you some pie or coffee cake."

"We're just stopping by to say hello, unless Jodie would like something…"

"No, I couldn't eat a thing. Travis fixed me a great breakfast this morning."

"Oh, really?"

Now that bit of news was going to be all over town, Travis thought. Good thing they were getting married quickly.

As soon as Jodie agreed with his plans.

Chapter Five

The second night in Travis's house was as quiet as the first, Jodie thought as she looked out the window into the clear, cool night. She wasn't as tired today, however, because she'd rested up from her flight to Texas. Still, she'd taken a nap after they'd gotten back from town, giving in to the demands of her pregnancy.

She'd have to be careful when she went back to work because she didn't usually have the luxury of napping in the middle of the day. Sometimes they worked from dawn to dusk, waiting for just the right light to achieve the art director's vision for still photographs, or repeating the same movement again and again for film shots. That part of modeling was tedious, but seeing the finished product usually made it all worthwhile.

Even though some aspects of modeling were stressful and occasionally boring, she loved her life. She'd love her baby, of course, and she was sure her career and motherhood would blend almost seamlessly. After all, hadn't her mother been a great role model for single parenthood? Jodie knew that she had many more resources than her mother had possessed nearly thirty years ago.

She'd enjoyed seeing where Travis lived. He hadn't grown up here, but he'd decided to make Ranger Springs his home. Why? She'd needed to understand more about him and to get a sense of the people he cared about.

He'd been a charming host, escorting her around the town square. They'd avoided both the Robin's Nest antiques and gift store, whose owner would be able to provide flowers and decorations for a wedding, and Schuler's Jewelry, where Travis said they might find rings, after Jodie declined to make an immediate decision. They had visited several other stores and establishments, where Jodie met many of Travis's friends. All of them looked at her with interest and speculation. Apparently he was highly regarded in this quaint little town. Just as apparent was the idea that he didn't bring many female friends to visit him here.

He'd gone into his studio to work after dinner, explaining he had some things to take care of on one of his jobs. But a few minutes ago she'd heard him below, walking toward his room at the corner of the house.

She'd come to a conclusion sometime between dessert and wandering the great room of Travis's spacious house. She had to talk to him *now,* before her decision churned in her stomach like the rushing water of the stream they'd crossed to and from town.

She stood, smoothed her hands down her French terry loungewear and slipped her feet into soft slippers. The time had come to face the consequences of her actions.

TRAVIS KNEW HE SHOULDN'T feel reluctant to approach Jodie. After all, they'd had no trouble communicating inside or outside the bedroom five weeks ago. Now, however, with her marriage solution and his marriage proposal standing like a brick wall between them, they seemed oddly disconnected. Strangely…shy around each other. He didn't know why; he didn't know how to fix it.

But he could try by going to her room again and asking for her decision. What if she said no? Should he try one more time to convince her? Or should he give up, contact a lawyer and try to secure legal standing with the child? Dammit, he just didn't know, and he hated uncertainty. He went with his gut feelings, took action and rarely regretted a decision.

Maybe a quick shower would settle him down. He'd worked in his office after dinner, distracted by thoughts of Jodie most of the time, then went to the barn for his nightly check of his horses and the barn cat who'd taken up residence around Christmas. Everything had been fine, so he'd returned to the house. The silent, seemingly empty house. Except it wasn't empty. Jodie was here, hiding from his questions in the guest room upstairs.

It's only been one day, he told himself as he shrugged out of his shirt and unfastened his jeans. Jodie needed some time to adjust, to weigh her options. Although she didn't seem like the kind of person who lingered and overly debated a decision, she probably wasn't as decisive as he. He needed to develop some patience where she was concerned, but dammit, she was under his roof, as tempting as ever, and she was carrying his child. How much patience could one man possess?

A soft knock sounded on his door, then he heard her voice. "Travis?"

Whirling around, he stepped into the bedroom from his walk-in closet to find her standing inside his room, larger than life in every way. More radiant, more beautiful and more uncertain than the woman he'd seen just hours ago.

"We need to talk," she said.

He nodded, not trusting his voice. "Come in." He gestured to the two armchairs in front of the cold fireplace. "I could start a fire."

"No, don't bother."

"It's no trouble." The fact that she didn't want to linger in front of a blaze dampened his spirits even more. She probably wouldn't even sit down. She'd just tell him that she didn't want to be married under his conditions, then leave.

"Well, whatever you'd like."

He breathed a sigh of relief, knelt on the hearth and used the gas starter to light the logs he kept ready inside the grate. When he rose, she was right behind him and, before he could turn, he felt her fingers on his back.

"You have a bruise."

"A little altercation with one of the heifers. I wanted her inside before the last storm. She wanted to play in the rain."

"Mmm," she said, her fingers tracing the spot. Lingering a while longer than necessary. A good sign, he hoped. Slowly he turned to face Jodie, capturing her lingering fingers with his hand. Pressing her against his chest.

"I've missed you," he said softly, as though she might turn and bolt like one of his skittish longhorns.

"I've missed you, too," she whispered, her fingers pressing into his chest. Her presence raised both heat and goose bumps as he inched closer.

"Ah, Jodie," he sighed, angling his head for a kiss. A real, passionate, heart-stopping, tongue-melting kiss like he'd dreamed of for long weeks.

She bolted, slipping out of his grasp before he could convince her to stay. "We need to talk."

He sighed, this time out of frustration rather than passion. "Of course. Let me get my shirt. I was just going to take a shower."

"I could come back if this isn't a good time."

"No, that's fine. I'll take my shower later," he said from inside his closet. A cold one, no doubt, when he remembered the desire in her green eyes before she'd stepped back. He returned, dressed. "Would you like to sit down?"

She nodded, then stepped closer and took a seat in one of the chairs. She looked vulnerable as she pressed her knees together and tucked her hands beneath her thighs. She took her lip between her teeth, which made her seem even more nervous than when she'd told him she was pregnant.

"Maybe the best thing would be to just tell me what decision you've made," he advised as gently as possible.

"Well, you're probably right. That doesn't make me any less nervous. I feel as though I'm making a decision that will affect my whole life. Maybe the most important decision of my life."

"I think you're right. I don't know what else to say, because I've already tried to make my points on why we'd be good together."

"You have. And you know I had to see the town, meet your friends. They're very nice, by the way. The town was...cute."

He smiled. "Cute? I suppose it would be to a cosmopolitan girl like you. No skyscrapers, no parking garages, no multilane freeways."

"Yes, but no rush hours, no stuck elevators, no rude people waiting for your parking spot."

"So true. So," he said slowly, "did the 'cute' town sway you one way or the other?"

"Actually, seeing you around the people who live here did more to sway me than anything else."

"Really?" He sure hoped that was a good sign.

"Yes. I—I've decided we should give marriage—a real marriage—a try."

"I don't want to *try*, Jodie. I want to succeed."

"Of course I want to succeed, also."

"Then we can't go in thinking it might not work. I've already been divorced once and I'm only thirty-three. With a child on the way, I want us to be a real family. A permanent family."

"All I can say is that I'm willing to give it my best."

"Then I'm not worried, because you're a very successful person. If you give our marriage the same effort you've given your career, then we'll be fine."

Jodie looked as if she was trying to respond, but she couldn't get any words past the knot in her throat.

Travis felt a little choked up himself. He was getting married. He was going to be a father. And he and Jodie still had a mountain of issues to overcome.

"I want to hug you, Jodie. I want to kiss you, but I feel as though you're holding back. Can you tell me what's wrong?"

"I don't know, Travis. I don't know how to explain how I'm feeling. I know that for two and a half days we couldn't keep our hands off each other. In January, it was like we'd known each other forever and were perfect together. Now I feel we're practically strangers."

"Obviously we're not strangers, since we're having a baby."

"That's what makes it so odd." She shook her head. "Like I said, I can't explain it. All I know is that we need to get acquainted all over again. We can't jump back into the relationship we had in Monte Carlo."

"I agree, but maybe we could start by agreeing to be a little bit affectionate. When we feel like it." And he felt like it a lot lately, especially with her sitting in his semi-darkened bedroom in front of a toasty fire.

"I can do that."

He leaned forward, steepling his fingers. "Or we could do a lot more, whenever you feel like it. I just want you to know I'm willing to cooperate," he added with a grin.

She raised her eyebrow and said in a chiding tone, "Oh, now you're willing to cooperate! After laying down the law about your plan versus my plan."

"I'm all for making us happy. Staying married will make us happy in the long run. Making love will make us even happier in the short term."

Jodie laughed, then rose from the chair. "I think I'd better be going."

He stood also, which put them nearly nose-to-nose. Travis reached out and held her shoulders. She seemed more relaxed now than since she'd arrived at his door. He wanted to believe she was happier now that the decision had been made. The uncertainties of relationships weren't good for either of them. A solid, stable union would provide the best basis for maintaining a marriage and raising a baby.

"Good night, Jodie," he said softly, then leaned closer for a kiss. He meant a simple parting kiss, to get them back into the affectionate mode. But the minute their lips touched, he felt the familiar fireworks he'd only experienced once before. Five weeks before.

She slanted her head and responded tentatively at first, then more passionately as their tongues met and their bodies melded together. Her full breasts flattened against his chest and his arousal pressed hard against her stomach.

Right where she carried his child.

The thought sobered him from the intoxicating kiss, giving him some measure of control when all he really wanted to do was guide her toward his king-size bed.

He eased away slightly, his breathing ragged. "That's a good start."

"Start?" she asked breathlessly.

"To being more affectionate."

"Hmm, affectionate. Yes, that's a start."

"Because I'm not planning for a marriage in name only. If we need some time to get reacquainted, that's fine, and perfectly understandable. But we really wanted each other last month." Unless he'd completely lost his ability to read Jodie, both of them still wanted each other thirty seconds ago. He took a deep breath. "I think we're going to both want to share the same bedroom very soon."

"I think you're right. We just need some time."

"Not too much time, though, right?"

Jodie gave him an enigmatic smile. "Good night, Travis."

"I'll wake you in the morning. We'll need to go to the county seat to get our marriage license, then I'll call Bretford House and make arrangements."

"Won't they already be busy for Valentine's Day?"

"Probably, but I'm not worried. They'll work us in. They have to."

"And I'll call my mother and publicist in California tonight and my booking agent in New York in the morning."

"What about your father?"

She waved her hand dismissively. "He hasn't been a part of our lives in twenty-four years. I won't look him up to ask him to my wedding. I don't even know where he lives, and frankly, I don't care."

Travis nodded, unsure of how to respond. He guessed that she had some unresolved anger at the man, but this wasn't the time to pursue his suspicion since she'd been so adamant that her father wasn't—and would never be—a part of her life.

"What about your parents? I know they're divorced, but will they both come?"

He thought of his socially active mother in Palm Springs. The last time he'd talked to her, around Christmas, she'd been pursuing an orthodontist. At least she'd get new veneers out of this relationship. And his father, still unhappily married to a woman he'd left his first wife, Travis's mother, for about twenty years ago. They lived on the East Coast and stayed busy with tennis, golf and mutual friends—most of whom were equally unhappily married.

If his mother came to the wedding, his father wouldn't. And vice versa. So he wasn't counting on his side of the aisle to be filled with kin, with the possible exception of his sister Kate's family. Unless her son Eddie was still sick with the flu, she'd be here. Gloating, probably. She'd always said he would get married again, when he met the right woman. Once she found out he and Jodie were expecting a child, she'd go ballistic.

"Sweetheart, I'm not sure who will show up on Saturday, but we're not going to let that spoil our day."

JODIE RETREATED TO THE relative safety of the guest room. She had plans to make that she hadn't discussed with Travis. Perhaps he didn't want to think about the complexities of weddings and marriage, but she had to consider everything. Such as having her dress and accessories shipped or packed for her mother to bring to Texas. Other than that, she didn't need anything else right now.

She would keep her condo for when she'd be staying in L.A. She might as well be comfortable. Besides, she loved the location and the view, so it didn't make sense to give it up for a marriage that still didn't seem real.

First, however, she should do as she'd mentioned and call her mother and sister. She was pretty sure her mother would come, but her sister Chelsea… Well, she might come if she was between relationships and would accept a paid airline ticket. Chelsea worked as a hostess for a trendy L.A. bistro, making enough to afford her own apartment and not much else. She usually had a high-roller boyfriend, however, so she enjoyed good food, expensive wine and many gifts. Jodie didn't approve of her sister's lifestyle, but she loved her anyway, and she wanted her at the wedding.

But before she could ask Chelsea to be her maid of honor, she needed to call her mother, who was still her closest friend. Her mother had taught her financial responsibility and self-esteem when the rest of the world seemed be saying she was too tall and too fat to find a good husband, which was the way to get ahead. Looking back, Jodie realized that wasn't necessarily the message she should have gotten, but while she was going through puberty and then learning about romantic relationships, that *seemed* to be the truth.

She dialed her mother's number on her cell phone, visualizing her at home. She'd probably be reading a good book, drinking tea and petting her lazy cat, Fred.

"Hello?"

"Hi, Mom. What are you doing on Saturday?"

EARLY THE NEXT DAY Travis and Jodie returned to Ranger Springs after going to the county clerk's office for a marriage license. They parked around back to avoid seeing as many people as possible as they headed for Schuler's Jewelry Store.

"Mr. Schuler, I hope you can keep a secret," Travis said to the smiling, dapper jeweler.

"I never let anyone know Grayson Phillips bought an engagement ring for Dr. Amy, now, did I?"

"No, you sure didn't," Travis said with a smile. "We're getting married on Saturday, so we need some bands."

"No engagement ring?"

"No time," Travis replied, putting his arm around Jodie. "We have to keep this quiet because my fiancée is rather famous and we don't want a bunch of reporters here before the big event."

"I understand. Let me show you some diamond eternity bands that I think would look lovely on your bride."

Jodie agreed and smiled rather stiffly. Travis wondered if she was thinking about the term "eternity," but he could hardly ask her in front of Mr. Schuler.

Although love was meant to last forever—at least according to the diamond ads—that's not what he was looking for. He did, however, hope their marriage lasted a lifetime.

Later that night they had dinner with Hank and

Gwendolyn, which was surprisingly comfortable. Since they'd all known each other before, they caught up on mutual friends and favorite charities and current events. Around ten o'clock Jodie began to yawn discreetly. Travis took that as his cue to get her home.

"I'm sorry I'm so sleepy lately," she said as he drove the short distance back to the ranch.

"That's okay," he said. "You're sleeping for two now."

Jodie smiled as she laid her head back against the seat. Travis sighed when he realized he'd be sleeping alone…again.

Chapter Six

Jodie's mother and sister arrived on Friday with her dress, shoes and a whole bunch of questions. While Chelsea looked around the house and sneaked outside for a smoke, Jodie helped her mother unpack.

"How can you be sure about marrying him so soon?" her mother asked as she unzipped her suitcase in the guest bedroom she shared with Chelsea. "You only met him in January."

"Well, when it's right, it's right," Jodie replied, grabbing some hangers from the closet. She wasn't ready to tell her mother and sister that she'd come to Texas because she was pregnant and was now marrying for the sake of her career. If she and Travis had been able to completely recapture the magic they'd shared... But they hadn't. Their memorable kiss on Tuesday night had left her breathless and wanting more, but they'd both been able to resist the desire.

Unlike when they'd first met. When they hadn't been able to keep their hands off each other.

"I know you think I'm marrying too quickly, but you have to admit that Travis is quite the catch."

"He seems to be." Her mother frowned as she removed a stack of underwear and a package of hosiery. "He seems almost too good to be real. Are you sure he's financially secure? Did you check out his credit report?"

"No, and I'm not going to. He's a very successful architect," Jodie claimed as she placed her mother's beige Chanel suit on a hanger. "He gets commissions from all over the world. When we met, he was in Europe, where he's designing a new cultural center. He does both exclusive homes and public buildings."

"I'm just saying that you can't be too careful."

"I know all I need to know, Mom."

Her mother sighed, holding a nightgown close to her chest. "I know what it's like to be so much in love that you make decisions…well, decisions that might be better made after some time getting to know each other."

"I'm getting married now, Mom. Can't you just be happy for me?" Jodie wasn't about to admit she and Travis weren't madly in love. That was the only excuse—except an unplanned pregnancy—for getting married so quickly.

"Of course I am. You just surprised me, Jodie. You're not usually so impulsive."

"Travis says he follows his intuition, but I call that being impulsive."

"I do, too." Her mother sighed and placed her beige pumps on the floor of the closet, next to the mother-of-the-bride suit.

"So he wanted to get married on Valentine's Day, and he pretty much swept me into the plans."

"I just hope you're happy with your decision in six months or a year. After all, you could have had a big wedding in the wine country, like you've always talked about."

"I know." She'd had her perfect wedding planned for years, just in case she found Mr. Right. An outdoor wedding in an arborlike setting, with all her friends and family. A huge cake, good wine and excellent nouveau cuisine. A beautiful photo to appear in all the magazines.

Well, she'd at least have some good photographs. She'd hired one of her favorite photographers, who was flying in this afternoon from New York. He'd make sure she had a wedding album she'd be proud to show her son or daughter someday.

This is your father, she'd tell her child. *Isn't he handsome? He's tall and well-built and sexy.* No, scratch that! She wouldn't be mentioning that to her child, no matter how true. She'd have to come up with a really convincing story, though, such as, *Your father and I felt an immediate attraction.* Yes, that would work—and it certainly wasn't a lie.

"If you really want to marry Travis, then I wish you both every happiness. That's all I've ever wanted for both you girls, Jodie."

She hugged her mother, smelling the familiar scent of Shalimar. "I know that, Mom. And I'm going to be happy. You just wait and see."

Chelsea burst into the room, bringing in the smell of

outdoors mixed with cigarette smoke. Not a good combination. Jodie wished her sister would quit smoking, but Chelsea always claimed that she'd gain weight—a fate worst than death considering how hard she worked to maintain a size eight. Even now, she claimed she was too big. *Men want thin women*, she always said. *Women admire you, Jodie, but I need a man around.*

Jodie thought her sister was mistaken. Without a man to constantly please, maybe Chelsea could discover who she really was inside.

"Bridal jitters?" she asked, her eyes alight with laughter.

"Not too much. Just a little mother-daughter bonding," Jodie answered.

"This is the first wedding for my girls."

"I'm not planning on another one, Mom," Jodie said with a laugh.

"No, but Chelsea might."

She shrugged. "Maybe. Anything's possible, but I wouldn't get your hopes up for Hugh. I just found out he's in debt up to his ears."

"That's no way to start a marriage," their mother said.

"Right. But he's fun. I'm going to keep him around for a while."

"Oh, Chelsea."

"Don't worry, Mom. It's not serious."

Jodie knew differently. Everything was serious for Chelsea until she discovered her current boyfriend's flaws. Then she moved on to the next…and the next.

"Well, at least one of my girls will be happily married."

Jodie hid her expression behind of big swallow of water.

"Right. Then she can make you a grandmother."

Jodie choked on her water.

"Careful, sis. I was just kidding."

"No problem. I knew you were joking." But what about when she had to reveal the truth? Was her mother ready for a grandchild? Would being an aunt make Chelsea more responsible?

But most of all, Jodie wondered if she would be a good mother…and a good wife. She would try to do the best for her baby, because each day she grew more and more protective of the tiny life inside her.

"WE NEED TO GET THE press release prepared immediately, Jodie. This can't wait until the local paper prints the story." Her publicist, Neil Dupont, had been bugging her all morning to help write the copy. She didn't want to deal with these details. That's why she paid other people—so she could concentrate on her job. And her job tomorrow at noon was to play the loving bride.

Jodie rubbed her temples and wished she could transport herself two days into the future, when the wedding and all that went with it was over. "Just make it brief. There's no reason to go into details."

"I think we need to mention the details. It makes the story much more romantic," her booking agent, Felicia Sparr, stated. Felicia was mid-forties, unmarried and practical almost to a fault. "We should fax this to our media contacts this afternoon, Jodie. I know you're rushing into this wedding, but we're just trying to help."

"I know, Felicia, but I…"

"What about the honeymoon? Can we mention where you're going? Just generally?" Neil asked.

"I don't know where we're going. Travis is taking care of that."

"Geesh, Jodie, don't you and Travis talk? This is important," Felicia stated.

She rubbed her temples again. "We need a professional."

"Exactly what I was saying earlier!"

Jodie looked up quickly. "I know! We can call Gwendolyn McCauley. She's Travis's next door neighbor and a public relations expert."

"No disrespect, Jodie, but a PR person from the backwoods of Texas? I don't think so," Neil said.

"Can it, Neil. Gwendolyn is the former public relations director to the royal family of Belegovia. She married Hank and moved to Ranger Springs. Now she does consulting for large companies in Austin and San Antonio. I think she's qualified to edit a press release about a very uncontroversial wedding."

Felicia raised her eyebrows and looked at Neil. "She does sound qualified. Let's fax her the release we've drafted."

"I'll take it into Travis's office and fax it myself, and I'll call her. Why don't you two relax? There's wine in the wet bar refrigerator downstairs."

"Are you sure you don't need us?"

"No offense, but I'd like to be alone for a while."

"We understand, Jodie. Bridal jitters and all."

"Right." What she really felt was closer to panic than jitters. Her stomach clenched and she felt slightly nauseous. She wanted to be alone, not surrounded by her business associates and family.

"We'll talk to you later."

Jodie nodded as they left her room. Alone, at last. She didn't want her mother to look into her eyes to read the lie. She didn't want to say or to do anything to show Felicia or Neil that this wasn't an impromptu love match. She didn't want to hear any more jokes from her sister about how this decision was totally out of character.

Well, maybe she wanted to be out of character for a change. Maybe she needed to do something impulsive.

Oh, like having sex in the shower with no protection, her little voice reminded her.

Okay, that was impulsive, but she and Travis both had been carried away. Their passion had burned intense and immediate. She'd never done anything like that before, and neither had Travis, he'd claimed. She believed him. Travis was honest. He'd had no reason to lie to her then, and not now, either.

Maybe she should focus more on his good qualities, she thought at she opened the door to his home office, and spend more time remembering those three magical days in Monte Carlo. If so, perhaps they could recapture the passion they'd shared…the passion that had created their baby.

The simple reality of their child helped center her in the chaotic world of press releases and relatives and weddings. With a sigh, she sat in Travis's desk chair, placed a draft of the press release in his fax machine and opened her address book.

"Hello, Gwendolyn. I have a favor to ask."

VALENTINE'S DAY DAWNED bright, crisp and clear. Travis went through his regular routine; feeding the stock, cleaning out the stalls of his three horses, adding water to the tank for his longhorns and finally making coffee for himself. And Jodie. He'd had her as a houseguest for five days now, but soon she'd be his wife.

He'd worked hard all week on the wedding, starting when he'd convinced the owner of Bretford House to allow the Valentine's Day wedding. He'd been booked almost solid for both lunch and dinner, Travis had been told, with loving couples who wanted a special meal. If the wedding were an outdoor event, no problem; they could set up tents. But not in February, when the temperatures during the day were forecast in the high fifties or low sixties.

Travis had compromised by inviting all of the regular diners, who were his friends and neighbors anyway, to the wedding. That made the guest list a bit more extensive than he'd planned, but what the heck? A guy didn't have that many weddings in his life…hopefully.

He'd arranged for Robin Parker, the police chief's wife and owner of Robin's Nest Antiques and Gifts, to do the flower arrangements and decorations. Nothing in "Valentine tacky," he'd told her, at which point she'd rolled her eyes. Robin was a former socialite from Houston, so she wouldn't have done tacky anyway, he realized too late. He'd been just a little bit nervous, though, and his friends had been understanding.

Hank McCauley would be the best man and Jodie's sister Chelsea was going to be the maid of honor. They didn't need any more people to stand up with them since this was a small wedding. He was grateful for that. His first wedding had involved a large cathedral-style church decorated in hundreds of white roses, hundreds of yards of white ribbons, hundreds of candles and seemingly hundreds of attendants. He hadn't even known some of the young women in the ceremony!

Well, this time would be different. Instead of not knowing the bridesmaids, he barely knew the bride!

They'd have a small ceremony with just friends and immediate family. Her family, at least. He'd called his relatives, but if the wedding were being held in a church, his side of the pews would be empty.

His father and his wife were leaving on a cruise to Bermuda on Saturday. His mother was recovering from her latest "procedure" and couldn't possibly be seen in public with bruises and puffy lids. She certainly hoped he understood, and made him feel as though he were inconsiderate for getting married without sufficient prior notice.

So much for his warm, loving parents.

His closest relative, his sister Kate, would have come in an instant but her son Eddie was still confined with the flu and her workaholic, often-absent husband Ed was once again on a business trip. Travis really regretted that she wouldn't be here. He truly enjoyed his sister and his nephew and had even purchased gentle horses so they would be able to ride with him when they visited.

But his friends would be here, just as he'd been at most of their weddings. They'd toast his happiness and really mean their good wishes, which was all a man could really want, right?

With a sigh, Travis took his mug of coffee to his studio. Since it was bad luck to see the bride before the wedding, he had several hours to kill until it was time to get ready. After the noon ceremony, they'd have a lunch for half of Ranger Springs. Then they'd leave for the honeymoon.

He was looking forward to getting Jodie alone. Maybe once they were man and wife, they could recapture the magic of their first three days together.

If they couldn't…well, it would be a long, long wait until the baby was born and Jodie hightailed it back to California.

THE PRESS RELEASES were ready to send, the photographer was all set up in the foyer, the guests were waiting…and Jodie was a nonfunctional bundle of nerves as she stood in the small back room of Bretford House.

"You look like a deer in the headlights," Chelsea complained as she adjusted the circle of roses Robin Parker had fashioned to go with the creamy dress.

"I feel like a deer in the sights of a rifle," Jodie responded.

"Not the sentiment I would have expected on your

wedding day, Jodie Ann Marsh," her mother said, folding her arms over her chest. "What's wrong?"

"Well, I meant with the media and all. Neil and Felicia have been after me constantly about leaking the story, getting the photos out to the right people and all that other stuff. This doesn't feel like a wedding."

"But you love Travis, right? I mean, he's a hunk and he's got money," Chelsea said. "His house is awesome."

"You sound like one of those teenagers in the movies," her mother complained.

"Please, no arguments today. I'm already strung too tight."

"Sorry, baby. I'm a little nervous myself. And now I'm confused. What's the real problem?"

"Nothing. Everything's fine. Everyone has done a re-markable job to get this wedding planned in only three days." The restaurant looked beautiful, like spring combined with winter, with all-white decorations of roses, ribbon, tulle and bare branches. Robin Parker had done a fabulous job by enhancing the fairy-tale quality of the old house-turned-restaurant.

Her mother took her by the shoulders and looked in her eyes. "Jodie, why did you really have to rush so? We could have planned a wedding in California or Texas, one that wasn't so frantic. Why today?"

"Didn't you read the press release?" Jodie asked, hearing the nervous, almost panicky tone of her voice. She had to conquer that. She had to calm down.

"That's for the public. We're your family. What the heck is going on?"

Jodie felt tears form in her eyes. Her throat burned and her head felt as thought it might explode from holding everything back. She couldn't do it. This was her mother and her sister. What had she been thinking? She needed to tell them the truth. She needed to do it now, before she walked out that door and told a lie to the rest of the world.

"I'm pregnant," she whispered so softly that she wondered if they'd heard. "I'm having Travis's baby and that's why we rushed the wedding."

"Oh, Jodie."

"Oh, wow."

"I should have told you before. I don't know why I didn't. I've been so confused and tense and worried about how this changed everything."

"Changed your relationship with Travis?" her mother asked.

"No! Changed my plans. My career."

"So this is all about that new contract you signed with the cosmetics company," her mother stated.

"Well, yes. Mostly. I mean, some of it is about the baby. I really want this baby."

"How much of it is about you and Travis?"

"Oh, Mom, I just don't know. I wanted a temporary marriage, but he wants one that will last. He wants to try to make this real and forever, and I just don't know if I can do forever."

"Do you love him?"

Jodie turned away to dab her eyes. She wore waterproof everything—mascara, eyeliner and shadow—but that didn't mean she would look good when she walked down the makeshift aisle. She could still look blotchy and swollen if she wasn't careful, and wouldn't that make a charming photo in *People?*

"He's really hot, Jodie," Chelsea said, placing a hand on Jodie's arm. "He'd be really easy to fall in love with."

Jodie nodded, her throat closing up again. Travis would be easy to fall in love with. Too easy, maybe. And maybe that was the problem. She didn't want to fall in love. She'd never really been in love and the idea was frightening.

Of course, she'd never seriously considered having children, either, and now she was. Anything was possible.

"Travis is very lovable, Chelsea." Jodie attempted a smile. "But he's taken. You need to remember that."

"Like I'd fall for a guy in Texas!"

"Like I thought I would, either," Jodie countered. Her immediate response surprised her. Had she fallen for Travis? Or was she experiencing a delayed reaction to their passion? A friend who was a graduate student in anthropology had told her once that great sex made you think you were in love. She'd claimed it was a biological reaction to make you procreate. Maybe that's all that these feeling amounted to—pseudo love produced from their wild weekend of immediate and mutual lust.

And if they started having great sex again, how would she ever know her true feelings? She was going to be married to Travis; she needed to understand how she felt about him.

"I'm doing the right thing, Mom," she finally said after getting her tears under control. "Travis is a good man and we're having a baby together. Getting married is the right thing to do."

"For you, the baby, or your career?"

"Hopefully, for all three." She'd debated that very question almost nonstop for days without arriving at a definitive answer.

"I want you to be happy, baby."

"I want to be happy, too," Jodie said, giving her mother a hug. "So we'd best put on our happy faces and get on with the ceremony. There are hungry people in the restaurant who were expecting a Valentine's lunch and got a noon wedding, instead. And Travis is probably 'chomping at the bit,' as they say in Texas. So let's finish up here and take that walk down the aisle."

"I'm ready," Chelsea said. "The best man is a hottie, too."

"He's also taken. Happily married."

Chelsea shrugged. "Are there any single men in this town?"

Jodie chuckled, glad to take her mind off her worries. "Some, but the number is dwindling according to the gossips at the local café."

"Bummer. Let's get this over with so I can get back to California. My own cutie isn't all that happy that I left him alone for the weekend. No telling what kind of trouble he might get into on his own."

"Sounds like a true romantic," her mother said with the dry sense of humor Jodie had grown up with.

She smiled, stood up straight and gave one final adjustment to her pretty, gauzy dress. Her wedding dress. "Okay, let's go."

Her mother rapped on the door, the music began and Jodie took a deep breath. The ceremony would be over soon, but then the marriage began.

She was as ready as she would ever be to walk down the aisle, but was she ready to be Mrs. Travis Whitaker? Or would she forever be Jodie Marsh, model and cosmetics spokesperson, girl-next-door and paragon to thousands of overweight teens and women?

She didn't have the answer, but she was going to search for the truth during the next few days, as she and Travis went on a short honeymoon trip. She needed time to think, although she wondered if she'd have much opportunity for mental activity with her "hottie" husband around.

TRAVIS STOOD AT THE END of the main dining room, his back to the windows overlooking the still barren gardens, and watched his bride approach. She took his breath away, filling him with a sense of awe that he was actually getting married again, a sense of responsibility for their unborn child and a sense of excitement over what would unfold in the next months. Life had become pretty darn predictable lately. Maybe a wedding was just what he needed to shake things up.

She wore a gauzy, cream-colored dress that flowed over her full breasts, nipped in at her waist, then clung to her hips and thighs as she walked. Her hair was swept back in a circlet of small cream-colored roses, then loosely curled on her shoulders when she walked toward him. She looked beautiful and fertile in a way that made him want her right here, right now.

Unfortunately they had the rest of the ceremony to get through, then a wedding luncheon for their guests and the rest of the town who had made Valentine reservations. Everyone had taken the change of plans well, maybe because they were getting a free meal, but more likely because they thought the idea of a surprise Valentine's Day wedding to be the ultimate romantic gesture. Just as he'd thought, this was turning into a PR coup for Jodie.

But he didn't want to think about that now. He wanted to enjoy the day, appreciate his bride and then get on with the honeymoon.

Hank nudged him, then gave him a knowing smile when Travis turned to face his best man. "I knew she was right for you," his friend whispered.

I hope you're right, he thought. He hoped a lot of things now, things he hadn't thought of in many years, like becoming a father. Becoming a husband again. But so many variables were up to Jodie. He could only do what he thought was best and see what happened.

Pastor Carl Schleipinger motioned for the audience to be seated as Jodie reached the makeshift wedding arbor Robin had fashioned of roses, some wispy fabric she called tulle and white-painted branches.

"Dearly Beloved," he began as Travis took Jodie's trembling hand in his and prayed for the best.

Chapter Seven

"I'm sorry your parents and your sister didn't get to come to the wedding," Jodie said as they settled into Travis's SUV for the drive to the cabin. He'd explained that on such short notice, and due to her public persona, he'd arranged for Grayson Phillips's cabin on Lake Buchanan, which was northwest of Austin.

They'd stopped by his house to change from his suit and tie and her dress into casual clothes. They'd also grabbed the suitcases they'd packed earlier, plus a cooler of food. Now they were heading north out of town on the state highway.

"That's okay. It wasn't a surprise that my parents were unavailable. I would have enjoyed my sister saying 'I told you so' from the front row, though."

"Still, I'm sure you would have rather your parents came to your wedding."

Travis shrugged. "Actually, it would have been very awkward if both of them came. They despise each other. Plus, my mother can't stand my father's wife, who is the age my mother wants everyone to believe she is."

"I'm sorry they can't get along. I grew up without a father, and my mother, my sister and I are very close. I'm so glad they were there for me."

Travis drove for a while, then turned to look at her. "Did you tell them about the baby?"

"Yes, earlier today. I thought I could keep it from them, but…well, I just couldn't."

"Why didn't you want them to know?"

"I guess I have a little of my rebellious sister in me. I didn't want my mother to think poorly of me, as though I'd made a stupid mistake."

"*We* made a mistake by not using protection, but our baby isn't a mistake."

"No, of course not! That's not what I meant. But in my family, Chelsea is the one most likely to forget birth control. I'm the responsible one."

"Nobody's perfect."

"Obviously. If I were perfect, I'd be a size eight and would always think before I acted."

"What makes you think a size eight is perfect? I think you're absolutely perfect for your body type. You're a tall woman. I hope this doesn't sound offensive, but I believe you're what is called 'big boned.' You'd be nothing *but* bones if you were a size eight."

"You're right that I couldn't get down that small without seriously damaging my health, but this," she said, sweeping her hand from head to foot, "is more than bones."

"Yes, and you look and feel very good that way."

"Why, thank you. I wasn't sure you remembered."

"Did you interpret my restraint for inattention?"

"With everyone in the house, I don't suppose I could blame you. Er, not that I've been expecting you to take any action. We had three good chaperones for the last couple of days."

"I know. I was beginning to feel completely overwhelmed by females of every age, type and shape. And then I thought about your publicist—whom you have to admit isn't the most manly man in the world—staying in the cowboy room at the bed-and-breakfast and I got even more amused. All I can say is that I hope we have a boy. I'm going to need someone to help even the balance of your mother and sister, and my sister."

"I didn't know you had so many women troubles."

"A man needs someone to watch football with, throw a baseball, teach to ride and rope."

"As if you couldn't do that with a girl!"

Travis shook his head. "Wouldn't be the same."

"I didn't know I'd married such a male chauvinist pig!"

"I'm just kidding. Of course I'd treat a girl the same. Or nearly the same. I probably won't teach her to spit, and she won't be able to pee standing up."

"Travis!"

"It's the truth, sweetheart. You're in Texas now. You have to learn to live and talk like a Texan."

"I'm a California girl. I don't think I can turn into a Texan overnight by signing my name on a piece of paper."

"I'm not asking for overnight. I'm just asking for a chance."

She smiled in reply, but inside she knew she wouldn't be turning into anything but what she was—an average girl-next-door who had been successful due to her talents and God-given attributes. With a little help from highlights, cosmetics and Sara Lee cheesecake.

Travis drove well on the curving roads of the Hill Country. The hills weren't nearly as steep or high as those that separated the flat beach area around Los Angeles from the inland deserts. There were more trees and water here. Even though spring hadn't come yet to Texas, many of the trees stayed green year 'round, giving the landscape a texture and color that Jodie appreciated.

Still, before long her eyes grew heavy and she rested back against the seat. The SUV interior felt warm and cozy. She couldn't fight the urge to nap, which had grown stronger in the past week. At this rate, she was going to sleep right through her pregnancy!

She jerked awake sometime later, her heart racing. She'd had a disturbing dream where she was lost inside Travis's house, where mirrored hallways went on forever and she couldn't find the doors. When she looked at herself in the mirrors, she didn't recognize her image. She heard Travis calling her from somewhere in the house, but she couldn't find him and ran and ran until she was exhausted.

She rubbed her temples with trembling fingers. "How long was I asleep?"

"About thirty minutes. We're skirting the western side of Austin right now. Are you okay? Do you need to stop?"

"No, I just had a bad dream. A silly dream. I'm fine." Slowly, her heart rate returned to normal, but she couldn't help wondering why she'd had such a disturbing dream now, when the stress of the last few days should be going away. She didn't feel threatened by Travis. Yes, he could be intimidating, but surely now that the marriage issue was settled, he'd calm down.

She fell silent until he asked more about her childhood, and then they talked off and on until he pulled off the four-lane highway onto a smaller road. Slowly the dream faded in the comfort of the SUV and the unfamiliar landscape. This area was a little more flat, but still held her interest as they drove by pastures and houses and an occasional mobile home sitting alone in a field. Cattle and horses grazed on the mostly brown winter grass, but they saw few people.

That was fine with Jodie. She'd been around his friends, her family and business associates far too much lately. She was looking forward to some peace and quiet on their honeymoon.

She assumed they'd have some peaceful time. They hadn't actually talked about plans. They hadn't even really talked about their sleeping arrangements, although Travis had said he didn't want a marriage in name only. Since then they'd had no time to get reacquainted. Six weeks ago they'd met and made love, even conceived a baby together, but at the moment she felt awkward and even a little bit tense being alone with Travis. Would they suddenly start sharing a bedroom?

"I think it's just around the lake, maybe a quarter of

a mile more," Travis said, cutting into her thoughts of their time alone. Their long winter nights.

"Good. I'm ready to get out of the car and get some exercise. How about a run before dark?" Maybe some physical exertion would alleviate the tension.

"Don't you want to get settled in first?"

"We can do that later. I feel restless."

"Did the doctor say it was okay for you to run?"

"Yes. Did you think I'd do something that was dangerous to the baby?"

"No, of course not. I didn't mean it that way. I'm not familiar with pregnancy, except what my sister told me before I insisted I didn't want to hear about it. Mostly I remember tales of swollen ankles, sore backs and sleepless nights, but that was later, maybe around seven or eight months."

"Ugh! That doesn't sound like something to look forward to. I hope this pregnancy is different."

"I would think you won't have problems if you're cautious and don't overexert yourself."

"I'm going to do my best to stay healthy, which means I need to keep exercising. And a mother's health is very important to the baby." She wanted her child to have every advantage, especially a good start in life. "So, how about that run?"

"If you're sure," he answered, his tone revealing some skepticism.

Well, she'd just have to show him that she wasn't going to suffer any consequences from moderate exercise and a normal schedule. "I'm sure. Don't worry."

"I'll need to get our suitcases into the house so we can change."

"I'll get the food inside, then we can hurry. It gets dark so early this time of year." She might not worry about a short jog, but she sure didn't want to run over unfamiliar ground in the dark.

"Look, there's the cabin."

The house was rustic and simple in design, set on a slope just above the lake with a great view. Gray Phillips had said it was his late uncle's weekend house. He and "Dr. Amy," as everyone called her, had ended their very first date here and used the cabin some weekends to get away. Jodie had been told it was private, clean and stocked with basic necessities—the perfect honeymoon cottage on short notice.

"Last one outside for jogging has to clean up the dishes," Jodie announced as she swung the cooler of food out of the SUV.

"Don't lift too much!"

She laughed off Travis's unfounded concern and entered the cabin. The cooler probably didn't weigh fifteen pounds. She lifted far more than that at the gym. She wasn't going to spend her pregnancy sleeping and getting flabby. She might need more naps, but she could still work out, run, bicycle and maybe even surf. She'd ask a doctor once she found a good obstetrics physician, because she didn't want to do any of her regular activities that might be harmful to the baby. Despite the way she'd laughed off Travis's concerns, she took her pregnancy seriously.

"Where do you want your suitcase?" Travis asked.

She stood in the kitchen after setting the cooler on the counter, staring at her new husband. The enormity of their situation hit her then, as though she'd jogged into a glass wall.

Where did she want to put her suitcase? And where did Travis want her suitcase? They were married. Why did he even have to ask, unless he felt as conflicted as she did about their relationship?

BY THE TIME THEY RAN along the road circling the lake and returned to the cabin, darkness had fallen. Luckily, he'd remembered to turn on the outside lights. Travis was pleasantly tired from the exercise and ravenous for food—as well as hungry for Jodie. She was more of a mystery to him now than when they'd first met. He found that exciting, but also daunting. He knew the intense passion they were capable of generating, but he didn't know how to set the mood. Not surprisingly, a sunny outdoor café and an idyllic suite in a Monte Carlo hotel was more romantic than a borrowed cabin in Texas, even on Valentine's Day. Even if it was their honeymoon.

With a sigh, he stepped into the shower. Jodie had told him to go first because he was going to prepare dinner. She was in charge of setting the table, she said. She wasn't much of a cook, having lived with her mother for so long. She'd traveled so much, she'd told him, that having an apartment didn't make much sense when her mother had a perfectly fine house.

When she was younger and working in New York, she'd stayed with her booking agent, Felicia Sparr, who was kind of like an older sister or an aunt. Jodie had only gotten her own place after her modeling career had taken off, she'd told him.

He took a quick shower, trying not to think about Jodie getting naked. Trying not to think about the fact they were married and on their honeymoon. Trying not to think about where she'd put her suitcase, since he'd left it in the hallway when she'd said she'd get it later.

All that "not thinking" wasn't doing his libido any good. Maybe he should have taken a quick *cold* shower.

He dressed in sweats and pulled on socks, but no shoes. He hoped Jodie wasn't expecting a more formal wedding dinner, because he'd planned cheeseburgers, chips and fruit.

She was in the kitchen when he finished dressing, unpacking the groceries they'd brought with them for a couple of days. "The run made me feel so much better," she said. "Maybe I haven't been getting enough exercise. Since I got back to the States, I've been in meetings and negotiations far too much."

"Maybe. I'm glad you enjoyed it, and I'm glad you didn't have any problems as a consequence. I'm not an avid runner, but I do it when I don't get enough exercise the old-fashioned way—through actual work."

"Is that one of the reasons you bought the ranch?" she asked as she placed a box of cereal on the shelf.

"Indirectly. I really wanted a place to put down some roots, have a place I designed with a studio and room for guests. And like I mentioned before, I was tired of cities."

"If I get tired of one city, I just go to another one," Jodie joked.

Travis laughed, then the smile faded as he realized she wasn't really exaggerating. She did fly around a lot. Of course, that would change now.

"Are cheeseburgers okay for dinner? We had such a good meal earlier that I thought something simple might be best."

"Fine with me. I'm not a picky eater." She dusted off her hands and smiled at him, her cheeks still pink from the cool temperatures and their brisk jog.

"Why don't you go take your shower and I'll get started? Will about thirty minutes give you enough time?"

"Absolutely." She straightened a chair on her way across the small kitchen.

"Jodie?"

"Yes?"

"The wedding was really nice and I just wanted you to know that everything's going to be fine."

"I hope so, Travis. I know you didn't want to get married again."

"I didn't *think* I wanted to," he clarified as he stepped closer. "The reality is beginning to sink in and I'm looking forward to everything a marriage entails. And I really mean that, Jodie."

She smiled shyly as he took her hands then placed them on his shoulders. She felt warm and smelled like the outdoors. "Everything, hmm?"

He kissed her then, her lips soft and full beneath his, her body warm and real as she leaned against him. The passion they'd avoided for days sprang to life as she wrapped her arms around his neck and pressed closer. His arousal was swift and hard against her belly.

"I'd better take my shower," she said breathlessly as she pulled away moments later.

"Good idea. Otherwise we won't get any dinner."

While the burgers cooked, he cut up apples and washed grapes, arranging the fruit on a plate. He felt very domestic as he prepared the meal for Jodie. In a way, he was also nourishing his child. He wondered if he should pour her a glass of milk, but Jodie usually drank tea or water with her meals. He didn't want to demand she take special care of herself—just give some reminders since pregnancy was new to both of them.

They would have to find ways to compromise. Even more important, they needed to learn about each other— the everyday things that married couples or even those who lived together took for granted.

He put slices of cheese on the burgers and warmed the buns, all the while wondering what condiments Jodie liked. What was her favorite color? Her favorite flower? There was so much he didn't know about her.

Just then she walked into the kitchen, all pink and adorable from her shower. She wore no makeup and looked younger than her twenty-nine years. Her shoulder-length hair was piled on top of her head, held by one of those big clips, and she'd dressed like him in worn yellow sweats and white socks.

"You look great," he said.

She tilted her head and smiled. "Thanks. I didn't know the sloppy-out-of-the-shower look appealed to you."

"I have very fond memories of you and the shower."

Jodie laughed as she grabbed a slice of apple and a few grapes from the table. "Can I help? I can fill the glasses with ice."

"Sounds good. I didn't know what you wanted to drink."

"Just water is fine with me. I drink a lot of water."

Within minutes they were digging in to their dinner. "This is great, Travis. The burgers are perfect."

"I'm glad you like my cooking. Helen prepares meals for me about once a week. I keep a few main dishes in the freezer, also, so in case you need anything when I'm gone, just look there."

"I'm glad you have someone to take care of your house."

"I travel, and even when I'm home, I don't want to spend time cleaning."

"I'm exactly the same way," Jodie said.

They finished off the burgers, then Travis took her hand. "When you have your things sent to the house from California, Helen can help you unpack. If you want to store any furniture, I have some empty rooms above the garage."

She looked away, picking up the last grape and popping it in her mouth.

"Does that sound okay?"

"Mmm," she said around the grape.

He supposed she didn't want to talk about moving. After all, that involved a lot of work, and she'd had so much on her mind lately.

They cleaned up the kitchen together, then Jodie wandered onto the porch to see the lake by moonlight. Travis followed her. A quarter crescent moon hung over one end, reflecting in the water like a postcard for central Texas. He hoped Jodie found it restful and pleasant here.

He stood behind her and put his hands on her shoulders. She felt so nice and substantial—he could even lean on Jodie if he needed to. She was a strong woman in more ways than one.

"We could stay a few extra days if you'd like. It might be nice to relax, get to know each other better," he said softly, unwilling to interrupt the mood.

Jodie turned her head, but continued to stand facing the lake. "I'd love to, Travis, but I have to be in California on Tuesday. I have a meeting scheduled in L.A. with the creative team for the cosmetics company."

"You're flying back there on Tuesday?" He dropped his hands from her shoulders.

"Actually, I need to go back Monday night."

"And when were you going to tell me this?" He heard the hard edge to his voice and didn't even try to hide his feelings.

"We've hardly had time to talk. I meant to tell you in the morning."

"After our honeymoon? Our one-night honeymoon?"

"I was planning on you taking me to the airport on your way back to Ranger Springs."

"Well, that's certainly convenient."

"I thought so."

"No thanks."

"Why are you angry? If you had bigger plans, you should have told me. I had no idea you were thinking of staying here beyond the weekend. After all, you called this a weekend getaway cabin."

"That's what it is for Gray and Amy!"

"How was I supposed to know that?"

"I don't know, Jodie! How in the hell was I supposed to know you'd run back to California as soon as we said our vows?"

"I'm not running back! I'm doing my job. You do remember why we got married, right? Because of my career!"

"No, Jodie, that's not what I remember at all." He felt defeated and angry, as though all his arguments for making this marriage work had been for nothing. "I remember that you came to me because you wanted to salvage your career with a temporary marriage, but I also remember we talked about making it permanent. About working at our relationship."

"And I will work at it, as soon as I get back from California."

"Don't bother on my account," he said bitterly. He turned and walked back into the house, letting the screen door slam shut.

JODIE HUGGED HER ARMS around herself, feeling the chill of the night air as well as the coldness of Travis's harsh words. He'd overreacted to the simple announcement that she had to travel on business. This was a short trip that was absolutely necessary. She shouldn't feel guilty about going back to California for a few days, but she did…just a little, because she'd upset her new husband.

She'd discussed this trip with Felicia and Neil, and she thought she'd mentioned it to Travis, but perhaps not. There had been so much going on in the past four days, she might have forgotten. That was no reason to overreact as Travis had. He should have been more understanding.

He'd run off before they could discuss the problem. Apparently he didn't want to reconcile their differences. He obviously thought she should think and act exactly like him. Well, that was ridiculous, since most of the time she had no idea what he'd think or how he'd react!

Cold gave way to heat as she became angry. Travis was being dictatorial and unreasonable. She'd agreed to this marriage because she thought they had a basis to build upon, but maybe they didn't. Maybe he wanted a wife who would stay at home and bake cookies! Well, he shouldn't have proposed a permanent marriage to a career woman, one who was willing to enter into a temporary marriage to save her career.

She felt like storming into the cabin and slamming the door, but that would be as juvenile and overly dramatic as his departure from the porch. She'd do the opposite and calmly find her suitcase, then locate an empty bed.

There would certainly be no wedding night in this frosty cabin!

Chapter Eight

When Jodie walked into the kitchen the next morning, the sun was high in the sky and the coffee was old in the pot. Apparently, Travis hadn't slept late since he'd obviously made this brew more than an hour ago. She hoped he'd had a perfectly miserable night, tossing and turning as she had because of their argument. Not that it was much of an argument. He'd walked out before they could really discuss anything.

She took a deep breath and told herself not to think about how he'd flung his hurtful words at her before slamming the door on their marriage. She was going to be civil and polite despite her anger and disappointment.

Jodie made two slices of toast and poured a glass of orange juice from the refrigerator. Just as she sat at the table, the back door opened and Travis came inside, bringing the smell of crisp air…and still emitting cold censure.

"I think under the circumstances," he said without even a morning greeting, "we should head on back to Ranger Springs. I'm sure you don't want to continue this fiasco of a honeymoon any more than I do."

"Fine with me," she said, attempting to keep her voice steady. She calmly buttered her toast and refused to look at Travis. "I have things to do anyway."

"Do you want to go directly to the airport like you'd planned?"

"No, I don't think that would look too good. We should probably go back to Ranger Springs. I'll drive myself to the airport and turn in my rental car."

"Fine. I'll go pack."

Yes, you do that, Jodie thought. *I'll just sit here and eat my toast. I'll pack up my things when I'm darn good and ready.*

The two-hour ride back to town was much less cordial and chatty than yesterday's drive to the cabin. Jodie tried to nap, but she was too tense. What she really wanted to do was to rage at Travis for reacting too strongly to her simple and reasonable need to get back to work. The cosmetics company wasn't paying her the big bucks to sit around a small town in Texas and eat bonbons.

She waited until she was about to burst, then said, "Look, Travis, we can't go on like this. We're supposed to be newlyweds, not mortal enemies. If you'd just try to see this from my point of view, I'm sure you'll understand why it's important to continue my career."

"I'm not saying you should sit around my house and do nothing. But giving us only Sunday and part of Monday together after our wedding makes it seem as though the marriage isn't important."

"Of course it's important, but you're the one who said

we're in this for the long haul. Doesn't that mean we have more than a couple of days to get settled? Why does that mean I have to drop the rest of my life to play the dutiful wife? For heaven's sake, Travis, this isn't the nineteenth century!"

"The point is that you should have told me."

"I discussed my plans with so many different people that I thought I'd mentioned it to you!"

"Well, you didn't."

"I know that now. I didn't realize it yesterday."

Jodie had nothing else to say, so she remained silent. Travis had a point, but so did she. If she started backing down now, what kind of marriage would they have?

TRAVIS SLOWED as they approached the turnoff for town. He probably should have gone the long way around to his ranch, but he hadn't thought of it. He hadn't thought of much else beyond getting them back home.

If he could just settle into his house, he could make things right. He'd felt that way from the time he'd planned the space. Everything was just right, from the size of the rooms to the appliances to the furniture arrangements. Rarely had he accomplished his goal as an architect as completely as he'd done with his own residence.

Church was just letting out as he drove by the town square. He saw several people he knew: Joyce and Ambrose in their sensible sedan; Robin and Ethan Parker in his new police department SUV; Thelma Rogers walking with Jimmy Mack Branson through the square toward the *Gazette* offices. The scene of his adopted hometown and neighbors was so ordinary, yet today it felt different because he was different. He was married—again. And this time to a woman whose career and independence were far more important than his position or wealth.

The damn thing was that Jodie only needed his name and a minimal amount of cooperation. She didn't need his emotional or monetary support. She didn't need *him*.

He didn't know how to deal with her independence. The women he'd dated since his divorce had catered to his every whim. They'd been looking for a husband for a far different reason that Jodie's. When he'd told them he wasn't available under any conditions, most of them had stayed around for the perks—travel, parties, gifts.

Looking back, he could see how some people might say he'd held too much power over them. How he'd manipulated the circumstances to suit him. But he hadn't felt that way at the time. He never forced anyone to go out with him, to travel or to attend parties. They'd gone willingly or he'd gone alone.

He didn't know how to relate to Jodie, but he had an idea that an apology was a good place to start. Still, he waved to his friends and turned right onto the farm-to-market road leading to his ranch before he found the words.

"Jodie," he started as they passed Ralph Biggerstaff, his banker, and Ralph's wife traveling in the opposite direction, as though they'd been to his ranch. He waved again, then took a deep breath. "Jodie, about the other night…"

"I really don't want to argue anymore, Travis. It's not good for me or the baby."

"I'm sorry. That's all I wanted to say. I overreacted to the news you were leaving so soon. And the reason I overreacted," he said, sucking in another deep breath, "is because I was having such a good time. I was looking forward to our already short honeymoon. I was looking forward to getting to know you…again."

As the road straightened, he glanced over at Jodie. She sat still, watching her folded hands and frowning. Okay, maybe he hadn't done a very good job apologizing. That wasn't a skill he used often. He tried not to get himself into situations where he needed to admit he was sorry.

But finally she said, "I was really angry at you, Travis, and I overreacted, too. I'm sorry."

"I suppose we need to start over yet again."

"We seem to be doing that a lot lately," she said with a slight smile.

"Maybe one day we'll get it right," he said as he turned off the road into his long driveway.

"Maybe." She sighed. "I'm willing to try."

They rode the rest of the way in silence. When he pulled around the house, he noticed Helen's car parked in her usual spot beside the garage.

"That's odd. She's not scheduled to work today."

"Maybe she decided to get caught up on some things while we're gone."

"I suppose," he said, but he wasn't convinced. Helen had come to work for him after her father, affectionately known as "Crazy Ed" because he'd suffered from senile dementia, had died a couple of years ago. Helen's daughter and grandson lived with her now, and being his housekeeper gave Helen just the right amount of work so she had time to spend with them.

When they opened the door from the garage into the house, the mix of aromas made Travis's mouth water.

"It smells like a church social in here," Jodie said.

"I think you're right. I guess this is what my neighbors have been up to while we were gone."

"I hope it tastes as good as it smells."

Travis silently concurred. He hadn't had much of an appetite for breakfast after their argument last night.

"What a surprise!" Helen said as they entered the kitchen. "I told everyone you weren't going to be home for a couple of days."

"Jodie has a previous commitment in California," Travis explained, keeping his opinion out of his neutral comment.

"Everyone was so happy for you, and to thank you for the Valentine's Day meal at Bretford House and inviting them to your wedding, they've been bringing casseroles, salads and desserts since this morning."

"I noticed Ralph and his wife—I forgot her name— on the drive from town."

Helen nodded. "The Biggerstaffs were the last ones. Some came before church."

"Is that why you're here?"

"Some folks asked me if I was going to be at the house, and I thought it might be a good idea to properly store any food they brought out."

"Thank you very much, Helen," Jodie said. "I'm sure

everything is delicious. I was just telling Travis that it reminds me of the church socials my mother, sister and I went to when I was a child."

"We have some good cooks in Ranger Springs." She turned to Travis and smiled. "Not Robin Parker, though, dear thing. She still can't cook."

He chuckled, looking at Jodie.

She smiled back. "I can't cook, either."

"You big-city girls," Helen said, shaking her head. "Maybe there's hope for you. Travis can teach you."

"That's no guarantee," Travis replied. "Ethan cooks like a pro and he can't teach Robin."

Helen shrugged. "Maybe he's not trying. He didn't take fancy classes like you did."

"Really?"

"My mother wasn't much of a homebody. Ethan, on the other hand, had an aunt who taught him the basics."

Travis sincerely believed that Jodie wouldn't be in town long enough to learn how to cook, but maybe he was wrong. He hoped so. She was a sensual person and he could imagine her up to her elbows in dough or dusted with powdered sugar or surrounded by ripe, fresh produce.

"Now that you two newlyweds are home, would you like for me to stay to answer the door and put the food away? Or would you rather be alone?"

Jodie looked at him and raised her eyebrows in question. "Whatever is best for you."

"If you don't have plans with your family, why don't you stay for a while? We need to get unpacked and settled in."

"Of course. I don't have any special plans this weekend."

Travis didn't say anything. Helen had been alone for a long time, he'd been told, but he didn't know her whole story since he hadn't grown up in Ranger Springs.

He carried their two suitcases into the house, then paused. Faced with the same dilemma as at Lake Buchanan, he wasn't sure where to put Jodie's bag. Was she ready to move into his bedroom, or was she still angry or upset?

"Maybe I'd better use the guest room for now," she said, obviously sensing his quandary.

"If that's what you want," he said, heading up the stairs.

She followed close behind, admiring the play of muscles in his long legs and butt. "What I want is to establish some sort of truce with you. I don't want us to keep on arguing."

"Agreed, but I thought we were going to have a real marriage."

"We are. Just give us some time to settle in."

"I'm not trying to rush you," he protested, pausing in the hallway. At her skeptical look he amended, "Well, maybe a little. But I really don't want us to get into a rut of not being…close. The longer we keep separate beds, the more difficult it will be to readjust."

"Nonsense! Maybe it will just make it that much better."

Travis leaned close. "If it gets any better than it was in Monte Carlo, you're going to need a new husband, because I'll be dead."

Jodie laughed and took her suitcase out of his hand. "Stop rushing me, Travis. Believe me, the wait will be worth it."

"Ah, so you are intentionally torturing me. I never knew you had a mean streak."

"I think you're torturing yourself. Ask anyone. I'm not a mean or difficult person."

"I'd ask someone, but I don't know any of your friends."

"You know Felicia and Neil."

"They work for you. They're biased."

"My mother and sister?"

"Relatives don't count."

"Well, those four nearly exhaust the potential candidates, because I travel too much to make a lot of friends outside of modeling."

"You'll have the opportunity to make friends here in Ranger Springs."

Jodie wheeled her suitcase toward the guest room doorway. "I'll just put this away so Helen won't think anything's up. Or not up, as the case may be. I'll see you in a few minutes."

Travis stood in the hallway until Jodie retreated to the guest bedroom. Her room for the past several days and still her refuge. She hadn't replied to his suggestion that she could make new friends in Texas. Why was that? Didn't she believe she was going to be here long enough to establish relationships? Jodie was being evasive and he didn't have a clue as to what she was thinking…or planning.

JODIE QUICKLY UNPACKED, placed her dirty clothes in the bathroom hamper and freshened up to meet the neighbors. Not that anyone lived within walking distance of Travis's house. Back in Newport Beach, houses were packed side by side to take advantage of an ocean view and the high cost of land. Even the smallest house with a view went in the mid-six figures. Her own condo had seemed outrageously expensive when she'd bought it four years ago, but she loved the view from her balcony, the short walk to restaurants and the beach.

Here in Ranger Springs, she doubted anyone had a security system. Unless you lived around the town square, you couldn't really walk to shops or restaurants—not that there were many of them to begin with—and the view... Well, she hadn't seen the countryside at the best time of the year.

Travis had told her that spring would come very soon to the Hill Country, changing the landscape completely. Flowers would cover the hills, grass would sprout overnight and the sky would be a brilliant blue with white cotton-puff clouds. The picture he painted seemed a bit inflated, but she'd have to judge for herself. She would have plenty of time to view Texas between trips to New York and California.

After brushing her hair into a ponytail, she closed the door on the guest bedroom—just in case Helen decided to have a peek upstairs—and descended the stairs. She followed the sound of voices to the kitchen.

"We're just so happy for you," Charlene Jacks was

saying. She stood across the large kitchen island from Travis. Two blond-haired young women, which Jodie assumed were her other two daughters, stood with her.

"I'm glad you could come to the wedding yesterday." He looked over his shoulder. "Ah, here's Jodie now."

She smiled at the group. "Hello, Mrs. Jacks. How are you today?"

"I'm just fine, and please, call me Charlene. This is my middle daughter Carole," she said, turning to a striking young woman in jeans, a Western shirt and a fake fur vest. "And my youngest, Cheryl." Cheryl resembled Kerry much more than the middle daughter, with shorter hair and a fresh-scrubbed appearance.

"I'm very glad to meet you. Kerry has told me so much about you that I feel I know you already."

"When Kerry gets a little homesick, she talks about family in very glowing terms. I remember things a bit more realistically," Carole said with a laugh.

"That's not true!" Charlene protested. "She's very grounded."

"Yes, she is, but you've got to admit, Mama, that Carole and I were a pain in the—"

"Now, Cheryl, don't start telling tales to Jodie. She'll think we're a bunch of hooligans."

"No, I don't, Charlene. I think your family, like the town, is charming."

"Does that mean you're going to stay?" Carole asked. "It's a great place to live—and to raise a family." Jodie saw her place a hand over her gently rounded tummy—something she'd missed until now because of the furry vest—

and assumed she was expecting a baby with her new husband. She remembered Kerry mentioning the wedding to Huntington Foods's CEO Greg Rafferty last fall.

"Well, of course I wouldn't expect Travis to move to California."

"No, he's a Texan through and through," Charlene added. "You can't get a Texan out of Texas for long."

"Hey, I'm right here!" he protested.

"We know that, honey," Jodie said sweetly. "This is just girl talk."

Everyone chuckled, then Charlene said, "We'd best be going. You two are on your honeymoon, after all, and here we are intruding."

Travis placed his arm around Jodie's shoulders. "No, it was good to see you. And thanks again for the cookies," he said. "It's always a treat to check out a new 'Ms. Carole' recipe before the general public."

"I hope you like chocolate," Carole said to them both.

"Love it!" Jodie had forgotten that Kerry's sister was the famous "cookie queen," as the media had dubbed her, whose cookie recipes were produced by her husband's company in Chicago.

They said their goodbyes, then stood side by side and watched the truck pull away. "Carole is going to have a baby, too," Jodie said.

"Really? I hadn't noticed."

"It was a subtle thing."

"Ah, one of those private female moments."

"Right. The thing is, I'm not ready to let anyone know about the baby, yet. If it's okay with you, let's just keep it quiet for a while."

"Sure. I understand."

"There's no reason we have to be specific about when the baby is due, is there? I mean, do you think people will come right out and ask?"

"I'm not sure. I've never been an expectant father before. But my guess is that they'll accept something fairly vague like 'in the fall.'"

"Good. When it's time to tell people, that's what we'll say."

"Fine with me." He looked back at the kitchen. "I hope we don't get much more food or we'll have to open a restaurant."

"We could always go for another jog."

"I have a better idea. Do you ride?"

"Not like a rodeo queen, but yes, I do."

"Then let's go for a ride. My horses are so well mannered that even my sister and her son ride them. I'll show you around the property—"

"The ranch."

"Yes, technically. It's not like I have to make my living selling cattle, though. I don't think I'd be very good at keeping up with a big herd or shipping them off to the stockyards."

"Ugh. I wouldn't, either."

"See if you have some leather-soled shoes and maybe a light jacket. I'll saddle the horses and meet you in the barn."

JODIE REALLY ENJOYED their ride in the pleasant temperatures on this sunny day. Back at his ranch, Travis had seemed different than at the cabin, as though the pressure was off. Of course, the atmosphere was different because they'd both carefully put aside any sexual feelings for the moment. She wasn't sure of his motives, but she needed time to think about how angry she'd been at his reaction to her work plans. He had seemed to accept her explanation and apology, though, so that was a start.

He showed her his favorite spot, a sparkling pool of water he said was fed by the underground aquifer of the Hill Country. The area was isolated and surrounded by trees, so she imagined it would be a good place to get away for a little R and R. Travis had mentioned that his friend Hank ignored the fence separating the two properties and used the spot frequently for a getaway with his wife Gwendolyn. He'd tried to sound disgusted, but Jodie thought his outrage was a bit for show. Travis and Hank were obviously close.

They'd urged the horses into a slow, controlled canter and skirted his small herd of longhorns. When he'd said he had cattle, she'd assumed Herefords or some other beef animals. But now she realized he raised the old-fashioned kind of cow that had populated Texas a hundred and fifty years ago, not the more modern varieties. The speckled, spotted and solid-colored animals looked perfectly at home on Travis's ranch. She didn't want to get too close, though, because of their huge and lethal-looking horns.

When her bottom and inner thighs got a little sore from the unaccustomed Western saddle, they headed back to the house. Her cotton shaker sweater and flared embroidered jeans smelled strongly of horse and had genuine wear marks and real dirt rather than the designer kind. Neil would have turned up his citified nose, she thought with a smile.

When they pulled up at the barn, she noticed a different car in the driveway.

"Who's that?" she asked as Travis dismounted.

Travis turned to look at their visitor. "Thelma Rogers."

"Oh, the newspaper lady."

"I wonder what she wants."

"If you want to go see her, I'll take care of the horses."

"I'd rather help you, then we can go inside together."

"Fine by me. I don't blame you for wanting to avoid the press as long as possible, even the local one."

"She seems very nice, and you said she didn't print the kind of articles that slammed people." Still, they would have to be on their toes and play the loving newlyweds.

"She doesn't. I'm sure everything's fine."

They unsaddled and brushed down the horses, then gave them a bead of hay each and turned them loose in the corral. Travis said he'd wait until tomorrow to clean up the tack so they could see what Thelma wanted now.

"If you want to put your arm around me or hold my hand, I just wanted to let you know it's okay with me," she said as they walked to the house. "I mean, to keep up appearances."

"Of course," he said, looping his arm around her

shoulders. "You've had a lot more experience than I have at pretending for the cameras."

She felt like stepping away from him, but didn't. Thelma could be watching from the darkened windows. "I didn't realize physical contact would be so distasteful."

"It's not," he claimed, stopping in the middle of the yard. "But I would like to put my arm around you or hold your hand because we both feel like it rather than because it's expected."

She looped both of her arms around his neck to keep him from escaping. "Oh, Travis, just get over it! We married fast and everyone's going to be looking for the reason. That's a fact. We don't need to keep bringing this up. Or maybe you just like to argue."

He pulled back and glared at her. "Until last week, I never argued!"

She smiled a little too sweetly and replied, "Well, you're making up for it. Just quit looking for some dark motive in everything that happens. It won't kill you to be nice to me, even if you are angry that we got married."

"I'm not angry with you!" His hands tightened around her waist.

"Sounds like it to me."

"Well, you're wrong."

"Smile, dammit. We may very well have an audience."

"What I'd really like to do at this moment is to forget all about Thelma Rogers, her possible interest in us as a couple and her possible camera lens."

"Oh, I'm sure you would. Then you could run away from me and—"

"No! Because then I'd carry you into the house and show you what married couples are supposed to be doing on their honeymoon!"

That floored her. She couldn't think of one coherent comment to his remark…and all it implied. So she snapped, "Oh, yeah? You and who else are going to carry me into the house?"

"Give me a break. I could carry you if I wanted to." He still looked a little angry, but the ferocity had left his expression.

"Well, don't try it. I'm not responsible for broken backs."

He grinned at that, then threw back his head and laughed. Moments later he smiled down at her and said, "Come on up to the house, Mrs. Whitaker, and talk to the press. I promise to be on my best behavior."

Jodie couldn't think of a thing to say as Travis took her hand and led her into the house. *Mrs. Whitaker.* She hadn't thought of herself as Mrs. Whitaker before. Mrs. Travis Whitaker. How did she feel about that name?

Was Mrs. Whitaker a different person than Jodie Marsh?

Chapter Nine

"Well, your story has already been picked up. The engagement photo I ran in Friday's edition did the trick. I can't tell you how excited I am to have the exclusive on the wedding photos. I thought about putting out a special edition, but I decided that since I didn't do that for Prince Alexi, I shouldn't do it now. So the photos will run on Friday."

"Exclusive for now. Our photographer will be releasing the official photos as soon as I approve them," Jodie reminded Thelma.

"Oh, yes, I know. But this time I got to break the story. That's very exciting for an old woman like me!"

"You're not an old woman," Travis told her. True, she had gray hair in the style of many grandmothers, but Thelma maintained a vitality that made her seem younger than her sixty-something years.

"Perhaps you could do a follow-up story on us later," Jodie suggested, which made Travis cringe inside. He didn't want or need publicity, but he'd taken on the role of a celebrity's husband when he'd married her yesterday.

"Sure," he said with as much enthusiasm as he could muster. "But nothing too personal, okay?"

"Not even for *Architectural Digest*?" Jodie asked, nudging his arm.

"Well, perhaps." There hadn't been a feature about him in that prestigious magazine yet, but there'd been some smaller stories about a couple of residences and one of his public buildings in Phoenix.

"I thought so."

"That would be good publicity for your business," Thelma mentioned.

"Yes, but I didn't marry Jodie to get a feature in a magazine. I'd just as soon we have some quiet time."

"Of course you didn't," Thelma said, patting his hand as though he were a five-year-old. "But the perks don't hurt."

Jodie laughed at that, the sound lifting his mood. He hadn't made her laugh lately. He hadn't even given her much to smile about.

"On the down side, I have to mention that some of those more aggressive reporters will be in town soon. Travis, I know you remember when Prince Alexi was in town that first time. This will be almost as bad as that day at the gazebo when he held the press conference."

Travis remembered it well. He'd stood beside Charlene Jacks and watched as the prince had told a huge lie to the world. As the cameras had snapped off photos, Alexi had told everyone that he wasn't with Kerry Lynn Jacks, while, in fact, they'd been driving around Texas and falling in love.

Come to think of it, they'd had to get married, too. That marriage had worked out well. Of course, unlike himself and Jodie, Alexi and Kerry claimed they were madly in love.

"We'll handle the reporters," he told Thelma.

"I'll get Neil and Felicia on the problem. Maybe they can make some arrangements so the press isn't just hanging around, waiting for a photo op." Jodie paused, glancing at him, then back at Thelma. "Also, I'll be back in California on Tuesday for a meeting that was already arranged before we decided to get married. I'll work in a few interviews there, to take the pressure off Travis."

After Thelma left with promises to call them when she heard from other journalists, Jodie turned to him from her place near the window. Sunlight gilded her hair and emphasized the curves of her figure.

"I'm sorry your life has become more complicated since I showed up last week."

"No, you did what you thought was best," he said as he locked the door and appreciated the calm of his house.

"Maybe, but I should have thought this through more before I said we had to marry. This isn't fair to you."

"Despite the temporary inconveniences, I'm glad you came to me. I want to be a father to our baby."

"Still, I feel—"

He walked up behind her and placed his hands on her shoulders, massaging away some of her tension. "Jodie, don't worry. Everything's going to be fine."

"Mmm, that feels so good."

"Come with me, Jodie. I'll make you feel even better."

"I smell like a horse."

He kissed her neck. "So do I. Let's get cleaned up together."

She looked back over her shoulder. "Like in Monte Carlo?"

"This is our honeymoon," he whispered.

She reached up and caressed his cheek, looked deeply into his eyes, then grasped his hand. "Come on. We've wasted enough time."

He led her through the kitchen, down the hall and into his master suite. A sense of urgency overtook him until he realized he was practically dragging Jodie through the house. He'd probably be able to think more clearly if his blood hadn't deserted his brain for parts farther south. He had to get himself under control before they got naked or he'd completely disappoint both of them.

She giggled, breaking into his chaotic thoughts. "And here I thought you might be a reluctant bridegroom."

"At the moment," he said, pausing beside the shower stall, "I'm an overeager bridegroom."

Jodie pressed close and looped her arms around his back, smiling seductively. "I do like a cooperative husband."

"And I do like…you," he said. He kissed her, absorbing her warmth with the traces of not-quite-springtime air and horses and leather. He smoothed his hands down her back, willing himself to go slow. *She's carrying your child,* he told himself.

But then her fingers found his belt and buttons and desire exploded in his brain. "Go slow," he murmured.

"Why?" she said, laughter in her muffled voice as she nuzzled his chest.

He knew she didn't want to hear him tell her one more time to be careful. To remind her that she was pregnant and her life had changed, no matter what she believed about being healthy and fit and practically indestructible.

"Come on, slowpoke," she challenged, pulling his shirt from his jeans.

"Lesson one on making love to a cowboy," he said, grasping her hands and tugging her toward the padded bench beside the big whirlpool tub. "Boots come off first."

Jodie laughed and pushed him onto the bench, then went to work with more enthusiasm than skill. Her levity and his sobering thoughts allowed him to regain some control. By the time she'd removed his boots and socks, and started on his jeans, he knew he willed himself to calm down, to be careful. One of them had to be…

He pulled her up when her lips started a path down his chest and abs. *Not a good idea if he were to go slow.* Instead he kissed her and started to work on her clothes, undressing her as efficiently as possible as she moved and wiggled and generally played havoc with his senses.

"Remind me to admire your bathroom later," she said, peeling herself out of her jeans. He barely had time to admire her long legs, strong thighs and curvy hips before she reached for him again. She backed him toward the shower stall, tugging his briefs down.

Within a minute they were both naked and breathing hard beneath the steaming water. "Just like Monte Carlo," Jodie whispered in his ear, nipping his lobe with her teeth. Shivers raced down his spine. His long-denied libido urged him to give in to the passion. To press into her as he'd done that first weekend and to lose himself to the rhythm she demanded. But he couldn't. *Go slow. She's carrying your child*, he silently chanted.

"Travis," she moaned as he pressed her against the tile, bent his knees, grasped her hips and eased inside. He concentrated on her pleasure with measured strokes and gentle pressure until she gasped and tightened around him. Not even then would he give in to her pleas or the demands of her body. Or his. He continued to go slow until he pushed her over the edge one more time. Only then did he allow himself to climax, holding her tight and drinking in the sound and feel and smell of their passion.

They washed in silence, both of them still breathing hard when Travis turned off the water. He sluiced water from his eyes and smiled at Jodie.

She was frowning back at him.

"What's wrong? Are you okay?"

"I'm fine," she said, reaching for a towel. "Is something wrong with you?"

"No!" He felt like placing his hands on his hips and demanding what she meant by that remark. Instead he reached for a towel and began to briskly rub himself dry. "I feel wonderful. I thought you did, too."

"Oh, I feel fine. But you…you weren't very enthusiastic."

"You're critiquing me?" He wrapped the towel around his hips and tried not to glare.

"No! Well, yes, but I didn't mean it like that." She wrapped the towel around her and tucked the end securely over her breasts. "I suppose I was just expecting a little more urgency. I got pretty carried away, but I don't think you did, and frankly, Travis, that just isn't like you. Or at least, the you I knew in Monte Carlo."

"Things are different now."

"Because we're in Texas? Or because we're married?"

"No, because we…because I needed to be a little more careful. Things are different. You're pregnant. We need to—"

"Don't say it again!"

"Jodie, don't be upset."

"Oh, Travis, how can we be arguing again, right after we…after the first time we made love since our wedding." She ducked her head, but not before he saw an unnatural shine in her eyes.

He stepped closer and wrapped his arms around her. "Jodie, holding back while making love to you was one of the most difficult things I've ever done. But I could never forgive myself if I let passion take over and I hurt you."

"Or the baby."

"Right."

"Travis, are you going to be able to think of me as anything other than a pregnant woman for the next seven months?"

"Of course."

She sighed, laying her head on his shoulder. "I want things to be like they were before."

He felt a great tenderness, a warmth stronger than the passion he'd experienced before. The intensity of his feelings surprised him, but he tamped down those emotions and focused on making his wife understand. Just as he couldn't allow himself to make love to her unchecked, he couldn't become irrational about their relationship.

"We can't go back, Jodie. We can only go forward."

"You're right, but—"

"We're going to work through these challenges. We just got married, and that takes some adjustment. We're both intelligent adults. We can overcome anything."

He said that to her with great confidence, but inside he wondered if intelligence and maturity had much to do with the confusing feelings he was trying desperately to keep under control.

JODIE LEANED BACK in the thickly padded leather seat as soon as the pilot turned off the seat belt sign. Flying first class was a luxury she appreciated now that she could afford the ridiculous cost. Cramming her tall, overly curvy body into a regular coach seat was torture. In a few months, she reminded herself, she'd be even more uncomfortable flying as her size increased with the pregnancy. Where would she be, she wondered as she placed a hand over her stomach, when she felt the baby move for the first time?

The past three days had been a roller-coaster ride of emotional highs and lows, of physical attraction and mental challenges, culminating with making love in the shower. Travis alternatively infuriated and intrigued her, to the point where she didn't know how to feel about him or their marriage.

Jodie put on her headphones to block out the noise on the plane. The problem was they didn't really have a marriage yet. They'd had a wedding, and now a wedding night. After making love, they'd dressed and gone on with making dinner, chatting and sleeping together in his bed. Legally she was Mrs. Travis Whitaker, but inside she was still Jodie Marsh, independent career woman.

She knew many people couldn't understand her need to succeed, but she considered her body and her looks as a tool. She didn't believe she was overly vain or self-absorbed. She took care of herself—her skin, hair and general health—because they were all important to her *profession*, not because they were particularly important to *her*. Although, she did have to admit, she was fond of the perks such as facials, massages, pedicures and manicures.

While she was in California, she'd devote two or three days to her career and the new contract, which would provide her with both financial independence and flexibility. When she got back to Ranger Springs, she was going to concentrate on her marriage, she vowed as she twirled her sparkling diamond wedding band around her fingers.

She felt a strong surge of emotion when she thought of her new husband. Travis had saved her career and she didn't want him to regret that. She also hoped that they could build on the renewed intimacy they'd started to share. But could she risk her heart when she knew Travis wasn't particularly understanding about her career? When he'd become angry several times over misunderstandings?

They were so different in many ways. She wanted their relationship to last forever because Travis was more than just her baby's father. He was her lover, her husband, and now the most important person in her world. Together they'd be parents to a precious new life.

She'd made a commitment to him and their child. Before she'd left, she'd become his bride. When she returned to his ranch, she was going to learn how to be a wife.

TRAVIS HAD TRIED TO concentrate on the preliminary drawings for the new cultural center, but his thoughts kept straying to Jodie. What was she doing in California? Was she getting enough sleep? Did she miss him at all?

"Probably not," he muttered. He hadn't been Mr. Charming much of the time, getting angry when he should have been more patient. He'd jumped to conclusions, which made him wonder why. He didn't think he was trying to sabotage their chances to succeed at this marriage. But if he wasn't, what was he doing? What had made him so touchy?

Sexual frustration, he thought. Being abstinent in the same house, on the same honeymoon, with Jodie had driven him crazy. Their last night together had barely taken the edge off. He was eager for her to return home so they could make more progress on their marriage.

Of course, he wasn't going to give in to the urge to go crazy in the bedroom. Not while she was pregnant. They would be careful, because that was the right thing to do. That didn't mean they both couldn't enjoy each other immensely. He planned to prove that to Jodie real soon.

He welcomed the phone call from Hank on Wednesday afternoon as a welcome distraction from work.

"You and Jodie looked pretty darn good in that photo Thelma took for the local paper. She was showing it around the café. You clean up real well," Hank joked.

"Gee, thanks, and this from a cowboy who smells like horse about ninety percent of the time."

"Wendy doesn't mind, and that's all I care about."

"Yeah, I'll bet." Travis knew that when Hank had fallen, he'd fallen hard for the English lady.

"But you didn't even get your picture in the tabloid. The one where they claimed Jodie was marrying some mysterious Texas millionaire rancher."

"Yeah, I saw that one. I expected them to claim I was a two-headed alien or maybe Elvis in disguise."

"Maybe they're going to say that Jodie is having an alien baby."

"What?" How in the world could Hank know something that private. Well, not the alien part, but the having-a-baby part. "What do you mean by that?"

"Oh, you know those stupid magazines. They're always claiming alien babies or alien abductions."

"Oh." He felt an enormous sense of relief. He didn't want Jodie to think that he'd blabbed their secret to his friends as soon as she'd left town.

"We wanted to invite you and your bride over to dinner again on Friday. Wendy's got a wild idea to do a traditional English meal. I'd just as soon grill a couple of steaks, but you know how she gets, and especially now, with all these food urges. I swear, you'd think kidney pie would just about turn her stomach. But no, she's got to have some!"

Travis chuckled. "You sure can't get that anywhere else in Ranger Springs."

"Nope, and probably for a good reason. So, can you come for dinner? I'll even get her to fix a roast or something more normal in case Jodie doesn't like British food. I don't want to eat all this stuff alone."

"I'm sure dinner that night will be fine. I heard from Jodie and she'll be home tomorrow."

"Good. It must be a real bummer to have her gone when you should be on your honeymoon."

"Gee, thanks for reminding me. I'd completely forgotten what I might have been doing instead of working."

Hank laughed, but while his friend formulated a snappy comeback, Travis began to wonder why he wasn't in California with Jodie. Why was he sitting at home? She hadn't invited him, that's why. Had she just not thought about asking him, or was there a reason?

"So about seven o'clock," Hank was saying.

"Can I bring anything?"

"I'd say a dozen hamburgers, just in case, but Wendy would box my ears."

"I hear you. Okay, we'll be there. If you think of anything you need in the meantime, give me a call."

"Sure thing. Pretty lonesome out there by yourself?"

"Goodbye, Hank." Travis hung up the phone, then picked up his pencil and drummed it on the desk. Where was Jodie right now? What was she doing out in sunny California? And *why* wasn't he with her?

Chapter Ten

Gwendolyn placed the platter of beef next to the steaming kidney pie on the table and smiled. "We're so glad you were available tonight. Having this meal with you to celebrate your wedding is very special to us."

"Thank you so much for inviting us. Sharing this meal in your home is wonderful," Jodie said. "I've eaten in so many different restaurants lately that I forgot what home cooking tastes like."

"Business dinners?"

"Yes. The creative team from the cosmetics company was made up of mostly people from New York City. A couple of them had never been to California, so they wanted to see everything. They were all in hotels, so they thought nothing of eating out. All I wanted to do at night was go back to my condo and fall asleep."

"And dream of your handsome husband, no doubt," Gwendolyn teased.

Jodie smiled and Travis appeared surprised when she grabbed his hand and squeezed it. "Oh, of course I was," she said. Travis gave her a quizzical look.

"Well, we should have a toast to the newlyweds," Gwendolyn announced. "Hank, would you do the honors?"

"Naturally, darlin'," he drawled. He poured wine into Travis's glass, then reached farther to fill up Jodie's.

"None for me, thank you," she said as she placed her fingers across the rim. "I—I've about wined and dined myself out this week."

"Darlin', do you want some of that sparklin' grape juice?" Hank asked Gwendolyn.

"That would be lovely."

He poured her some substitute wine. Jodie realized this was her way to keep them from becoming too suspicious and still join in the toast. "I've always wanted to try nonalcoholic wine."

"Hank, please pour Jodie some."

Once they had their glasses filled, Hank raised his. "To my best friend Travis and his lovely bride Jodie. Darlin', you're a wonderful addition to our little town. Wendy and I wish you both every happiness for many, many years."

They clinked glasses and sipped their drinks amid smiles and good wishes. Gwendolyn passed the carving knife and fork to Hank to do the honors, and soon their plates were full of her traditional English dinner fare.

After the meal Hank helped Gwendolyn clear the table, insisting Jodie sit down and relax.

"Have you ever had kidney pie before?" she leaned close and asked Travis.

"No, can't say that I have. It's…different."

Jodie chuckled softly. "I don't think I'll develop a craving for it."

"Thank goodness," he said in relief. "Pickles and ice cream are bad enough."

"I'm hoping to develop a craving for cookies and ice cream."

"Good plan."

Gwendolyn carried in an English trifle and placed it in the center of the table. "My crowning achievement. I do love a good trifle."

"You're not the only one," Jodie said. "This looks delicious."

"Before we have dessert, we'd like to ask you something, Travis." Gwendolyn glanced at Hank and he smiled reassuringly. "You know we are having a baby this summer. We would be most honored if you would agree to be our child's godfather."

"WHAT A LOVELY DINNER," Jodie said later as they arrived back at Travis's house. She placed her pashmina shawl and purse on the granite countertop of the bar that separated the kitchen and great room.

"I'm having a hard time thinking of myself as a godfather. It seems like just yesterday that Hank and I were in college together, but then, I know it's been…gosh, twelve or thirteen years. That's a long time."

"Are you having a hard time thinking of yourself as a father?" she asked.

"I suppose it doesn't seem real yet. I mean, the pregnancy is very real, but being a father…that's a bit more abstract. Besides, we can't tell anyone." He paused. "That probably doesn't sound too good, but I'm just being honest. I know that when you start showing and we can tell the world that we're expecting, everything will progress rapidly from there."

"Of course." Still, she felt a tiny bit disappointed because she couldn't publicly celebrate her pregnancy, as Gwendolyn could. She hadn't thought of things like godparents and nurseries and layettes. That didn't mean she wouldn't start considering those soon. She was simply looking forward to her baby more than the "stuff" that went with parenting.

She had confidence that she would be a good mother. After all, she'd had wonderful role models in her own mother and grandmother. But she didn't feel motherly yet. She felt as she always did—confident, relatively happy and excited about the future.

The difference was, she realized suddenly, that the future had always been hers alone. Decisions *she* made. Events that happened to *her*. Now she would be responsible for another life. And if she and Travis stayed married, the future would be vastly more complicated with his goals and dreams, likes and dislikes, general health and personality traits.

"I'm sorry, Jodie. I didn't mean to make you sad."

She jerked her gaze up from staring at the pattern in the black, brown and white granite. "No, that's okay. I was just thinking. You're right. Having a baby means adjusting our thinking, not just our lives."

He came up to her and placed his arm around her shoulders. He felt so good and warm, so solid and stable. She leaned into him. For just a moment. Not that she needed a man to lean on, she told herself as she closed her eyes and sighed.

"You're exhausted," he whispered against her hair.

"Yes." Travis smelled so good. Whatever fragrance he wore smelled different on him than on anyone else. Not only had he been blessed with fantastic good looks and a great physique, but he'd also been given terrific body chemistry.

"We could go to bed. We don't have to do anything. You could sleep beside me."

"Hmm," she murmured, not believing for a moment that they could lie beside each other all night and not do something. She didn't want to make love again until she was sure they could recapture the magic they'd shared when they'd made this baby. Travis was too considerate a lover to ignore the fact she was tired and just a tiny bit maudlin.

"It might be better if I got a good night's sleep tonight. I have an upset stomach from the rich food."

Travis sighed and kissed her forehead. "I understand."

"We can sleep together tomorrow night," she offered.

"Jodie, really, I understand. You need your rest, especially after what you said about your trip. No wonder you're exhausted."

"I'll be fine in the morning."

"Still, you need to take care of yourself."

Jodie took a deep breath. "Good night, Travis."

"THEY'RE HERE!"

Travis inwardly groaned, but he didn't let his displeasure show. Jodie certainly wouldn't appreciate his thoughts about the people who populated her world. "Thanks for the info, Thelma. We'll see you around."

He hung up the phone and turned to his wife, who was sitting at the breakfast bar, sipping orange juice. "What did Thelma want?"

"To let us know the reporters are in town, hoping for an interview with you. With us."

"Oh. Well, that's to be expected. I talked to a few of the print journalists I know in California and posed for a few photos for them. I imagine the ones who showed up here are the second tier and the bottom feeders. They're probably looking for some sensational story." She paused and looked up at him. "No one in town has any sensational stories about you, do they?"

Travis chuckled at the idea of someone digging up dirt on him. "I don't think they'll hear anything derogatory about me." Even if they talked to his parents, they wouldn't dig up any "dirt." His family was dysfunctional, not criminal.

"Oh, good."

"Why? Would you have decided I wasn't a good candidate for husband and father?"

"Probably not, unless the stories were bad enough and they were true."

"How would you know?" he asked, getting more irritated by the minute. She thought she should have checked him out better?

"If you'd done anything illegal and been convicted, I could have found out," she answered defensively.

"Why didn't you just call a private investigator?"

She slammed her empty glass down on the bar. "Maybe I just didn't have time!"

"You should have taken time if you were worried about your future husband and the father of your child. Come to think of it, maybe you should have checked me out before you slept with me."

"Travis! How can you say such a thing?"

"I don't know, Jodie. Maybe because you're the one who brought up the subject of asking around town about my character."

"I've hurt your feelings."

"No, you've… Well, never mind. I'm angry that you even thought I could be hiding something reprehensible. That you thought I might be a criminal or just a low-life with secrets to hide."

"I didn't think that about you!"

"No? Then why did you say that you should have asked around? If you trusted me, you wouldn't say such a thing."

"I don't know why I said that. I do know that I don't think of you that way, but you are somewhat of a mystery. Your own parents didn't come to our wedding. You didn't grow up here, although you have friends you've known for a long time. You haven't told me much of your past, so that makes me wonder why." She took a deep breath, her eyes glassy with unshed tears. "I trust you, Travis, but I don't know you very well."

He turned away from the breakfast bar and cursed. Dammit, she had a point. They didn't know each other well. Looking back on last month, it seemed as though they'd talked a lot. But since she'd arrived in Ranger Springs, they hadn't discussed their pasts as much as their future.

"Look, I don't have any big secrets. Hell, I don't even have any little secrets! I'll be glad to answer any questions you have about my past."

"Can't we just talk about our childhoods? Our college years or whatever? I don't want to interrogate you and I don't particularly want you to question me on specifics. That's not what married couples do, is it?"

He thought back to his own marriage. They hadn't interrogated each other—they hadn't been interested enough to even think of it. "No, I suppose not, although I don't have a lot of good references for what married couples normally do."

"If you don't have good memories or good role models in your parents, for heaven's sake, think about Hank and Gwendolyn. Ethan and Robin. Charlene Jack's daughters and their husbands. Surely they would be better examples."

"Yes, they would, but I try not to imagine my friends in such intimate situations in their married lives."

"Really? Because I have to tell you, girls think about those things all the time."

He stood there and stared at her, his anger gone as he imagined Jodie and her friends gossiping and speculating. The image seemed so…ordinary. So non-glamorous, non-supermodel, non-celebrity.

"I think your observation proves the point that men and women are entirely different."

"Well, duh!"

Travis laughed at her cocky comeback. "Okay, I understand. We'll talk. We'll communicate. Isn't that the proper term?"

"I don't know about proper, but it sounds like a good idea to me."

"Which brings me back to the point of the reporters in town. What should we do about them? I suppose ignoring them until they go away isn't going to work."

"No, it won't. The smartest thing is to let them know when we're going to be available. Provide them with a photo opportunity in town, or at the ranch if you'd like."

"No, I wouldn't like that."

"Then we'd better give them some photos soon or they'll be here ringing your front doorbell until the law runs them off."

"As much as I'm not looking forward to this, we'll set up some interviews or photo ops or whatever you think is best. If I need to, I'll hire some security to keep the reporters off the ranch. I don't want them out here bothering us. We have enough to deal with right now without having Peeping Toms running around."

"That sounds like a good plan. I think I'll have Neil fly out tomorrow to take care of some of these details."

"Whatever you think is best."

"In the meantime, don't talk to them, even if they approach you. Just tell them you have no comment at this time. They'll keep bugging you, but by then we'll have our plan in place."

"Sounds good to me." He paused and watched Jodie sitting here in his kitchen, sunshine from the skylight gilding her hair. "While these reporters have us in hiding, what should we do?"

A spark of interest—did he dare hope sexual excitement?—flared in Jodie's eyes. Then she said a bit breathlessly, "I guess we should do what we've been talking about—get to know each other."

Chapter Eleven

Jodie called Neil in Los Angeles, then Thelma at the *Springs Gazette* office. The older lady swore she didn't mind coordinating a photo session and interview for Travis and Jodie tomorrow at the gazebo in the town square. Fortunately the weather was warm for the third week of February, so they could get some sunny, outdoor shots.

"I called Gray Phillips, who had some security contacts," Travis informed her. "I've arranged for two guards to watch the entrance to the property if we need them. I also called Ethan Parker to alert him to what I'd done, just in case he gets a call."

"Good idea. I'm sure there won't be a problem, but it's nice you're being careful."

"Thanks," he said, looking a little surprised that she'd complimented him. She supposed she hadn't done enough of that since they'd gotten married, but it was one step in her goal of becoming a good wife.

She needed to be good after she'd messed up earlier. She hadn't realized it at the time, but she'd really insulted Travis when she'd questioned his background. She had to be more careful, not only in what she said, but in what she thought about her new husband. She knew he was an honorable man—she shouldn't have wondered out loud if he had any skeletons in his closet. After all, they were already married.

"Neil will be here later tonight. He can answer any background questions the reporters might have."

"Is he staying with us?" Travis asked with a little trepidation.

Jodie chuckled. "No, he's booked into the Robin's Nest B and B in the cowboy room again."

"I'll bet he just loves that," Travis remarked with dry wit.

"Now don't be that way. Just because Neil is the man least likely to ever be a cowboy is no reason to tease."

"I'm not teasing."

Jodie carried her coffee cup into the kitchen. "What do you want to do today?" she asked carefully.

"I have a few chores, then I'm available for whatever you'd like."

"We could take a drive. I'd like to see more of the area."

"We'd almost have to go out of town. The reporters might find us."

"That's true. How about San Antonio or Austin? They aren't too far and I've never had a chance to visit there before."

"Sounds good. Let's go to San Antonio. We can have lunch on the Riverwalk."

"Okay. I'll dress down so no one will recognize me, not that it's usually a problem. Is casual okay?"

"Perfect. You can wear jeans almost anywhere along the Riverwalk."

"Okay then, I'll be ready whenever you are."

She turned to leave, but Travis gently tugged on her arm. "What?"

"This will give us more time to talk. I really don't have any secrets to hide, Jodie. I just haven't had that much of a memorable life."

"I'll bet you're wrong."

"I enjoy leading a very uneventful life. I'm not much for highs and lows."

"That's what makes life interesting."

"See, that's one way we're different. But I'm beginning to think that differences can make a relationship more interesting."

Jodie smiled slowly. "Good. I like that."

He smiled in reply, then leaned closer. "I'll see you soon." Then he kissed her, quickly but thoroughly, making her head swim. He turned away and walked toward the back door, as though he kissed her every time they parted. As though this were one of those little rituals married couples performed and expected.

Now that was something she could get used to.

THEY LUNCHED OUTDOORS at the Little Rhein Steakhouse, which overlooked a bend in the river that wound through San Antonio. Tourists and some downtown workers strolled along the flat, worn rock walkways that went right up to the water. Travis had always liked San Antonio, but the city was too large to make his residence. He truly wanted small-town life and Ranger Springs was perfect because he could visit two larger cities with a short drive.

"You know what I need? A latte. Ranger Springs needs a Starbucks," Jodie announced after finishing her meal.

"I don't see that happening in the near future."

"I suppose I could buy an espresso machine and learn how to use it."

"We could do that. In the meantime," he asked, "would you like to have some coffee here and talk? I'll tell you anything you'd like to know."

"Sure. That sounds good."

He motioned the waiter over, gave their orders and turned back to Jodie. "For someone who's concerned about how much we don't know about each other, you're not very pushy."

"Pushing you into talking isn't my goal. Having a conversation is."

"Hmm, I didn't think of it that way."

"Didn't you and your first wife talk?"

"Not very much. Not in depth. She talked a lot. I listened. She wasn't very interested in my background once she realized my mother wasn't going to be available to impress her friends."

"Your mother? Why?"

"My mother was an actress in the sixties. She wasn't extremely well known, but you might have seen her in some old movies and television shows. She was on one of the last episodes of the original *Star Trek* series. Her stage name was Shonda Malloy."

"I'm sorry, but I've never heard of her. What was her real name?"

"Rhonda Malkovitz from Scranton, Pennsylvania." Travis shook his head. "Hers was a typical Hollywood story. She'd been in several high school productions and did some local theater. Everyone said how wonderfully talented and beautiful she was, so she went to Hollywood to become the next Marilyn Monroe or Grace Kelly."

"So I take it what was extraordinary in Scranton wasn't as special in Hollywood?"

"Right. She did get work, although sometimes when she talks about the early years, I wonder exactly what she had to do to get roles. What kind of jobs she had to take to make ends meet between casting calls."

"There are still a lot of young women like that, not only in Hollywood, but in New York. The typical waitress-slash-actress or waitress-slash-model. I've met quite a few in my years."

"Oh, like you're so old," he teased, relieved to be talking about something other than his mother's unhappy early years.

"Well, no, but I am a veteran. I've been modeling since I was sixteen, although at the time I was trying to be much smaller. I got some jobs as a size eight, but even as a teenager, I was five feet, ten inches and pushing a hundred and fifty pounds."

"That doesn't seem like too much for being that tall."

"Not in the real world, but in modeling, it's way too fat."

"You're not fat. You're…substantial. Like a well-built house. Skinny women, especially ones who have had plastic surgery, are like flimsy tract houses. The fake stucco might look good for a while, but doesn't last."

"Gee, thanks again, I think," she said with a quirky smile. "I'm glad to know my stucco will hold up over time."

"I suppose comparing you to a structure isn't all that romantic."

"That's okay, I think I see your point. Being married to an architect is a new experience." She took a sip of her coffee. "So, back to your mother. I take it she didn't make a career being a Hollywood actress."

"No, she met my father when he was in Los Angeles. He'd decided to invest some of his oil profits in a film a friend of his was developing. He and my mother were introduced by mutual friends—"

"Much like we were," Jodie commented.

"Yes, except we were more…equal. She was struggling to make it and he offered her wealth and prestige. They were married shortly thereafter in Midland, Texas, which was his hometown." Travis shook his head, remembering the crying, the threats and the anger that had permeated his childhood. "She hated it there."

"Not exactly Hollywood, I take it."

"No, far from it. Midland and Odessa are two oil towns located in West Texas. The land is flat and the people are very down to earth. The novelty of a Hollywood actress marrying an oil baron soon wore off." His mother had expected adoration and deference, which he later realized came from deep-seated insecurity. Jodie, on the other hand, was the least insecure person he knew.

"By then she was pregnant with me, though, so she was stuck."

"I'm sorry she felt that way. Where is your mother living now?"

"Palm Springs, looking for husband number three."

"And you said your life wasn't interesting."

He smiled in reply. "I haven't even gotten to my father yet."

"What's he like?"

"He's unhappily married to a trophy wife who wants to look as though she's twenty-nine forever."

"How sad."

"For my father, too. He has to foot the bills."

"Oh, Travis, surely you see there's more to it than that. Any woman who worries so much about looking older probably has low self-esteem."

"We'll just have to agree to disagree on this one," he said.

"Okay, I'll compromise by waiting until I meet her to form my final opinion. That is, if I ever do meet her."

"Of course you'll meet her. We can't avoid them forever."

"Travis Whitaker, you have a cynical nature I never really appreciated before."

"I'm glad you're seeing some of my good qualities for a change," he joked.

He paid the restaurant tab, then took Jodie's hand as

they made their way down the stone steps to the walk. In February, in the middle of the afternoon, there weren't nearly as many people as there were during the weekends in the spring, summer or fall. They didn't get jostled as they strolled beside each other. Walking side by side, holding hands with his wife, was rather nice, Travis thought.

"This time next year, we'll be pushing one of those monster baby strollers," he said as they walked past an Irish pub that had been a fixture on the Riverwalk for years.

"Ugh! And here I am always complaining about those things when I'm out shopping. They take up an entire aisle."

"Yes, but I imagine they're very convenient for hauling around all the baby's stuff."

"I suppose," she sighed.

Travis felt surprised that Jodie wasn't more excited about the baby trappings. Didn't women ooh and ahh over cute little clothes and gadgets? He'd seen that often enough in his sister Kate. He'd had the misfortune of arriving at her house during a baby shower for Eddie. He nearly shuddered at the memory of all those women squealing over the remnants of pink-, blue- and yellow-wrapped packages. The living room looked as though a Hallmark store had exploded.

"So," he said, taking advantage of the quiet camaraderie to expand on the idea of the baby, "I thought you might want to call Robin Parker to talk about decorating one of the guest rooms for a nursery."

"I suppose. She's certainly convenient."

"And she does nice work. She's also from Houston. Her family is wealthy, from what I've heard, and she had a bit of culture shock when she came to Ranger Springs. You two probably have a lot in common."

"Maybe."

Travis felt his frustration growing. Jodie hadn't jumped on the idea of the baby things or decorating. What would get her excited about the pregnancy and moving to his home?

"Robin did a great job decorating Bretford House for our wedding."

"Yes, she did, and on such short notice. I don't know how she pulled that off," Jodie commented as she looked up at the trees and architecture along the Riverwalk.

"Ethan said she uses things that are already there or that are important to the client." He paused, stopping beneath one of the arched stone bridges, and gathered both her hands in his. "That's why it's important to pick out a room you like. Or you may even have some things from your childhood that could inspire a theme or a color scheme. Maybe you'll discover a theme after your things arrive from California."

"I'll think about it, Travis. We have months before we need to have a room ready."

He looked deep into her eyes. "What if the baby comes early or you have some problems where you don't feel like working with a decorator? We might not have as much time as you'd think."

She looked at him with fondness, but also patient

skepticism. "Nothing is going to happen to me. And I doubt this baby is coming early. If anything, as a first pregnancy it may be late."

He felt like frowning, but tried very hard to keep his expression neutral as they once again strolled along the walkway. "Still, I'd rather get the process going."

"We agreed not to tell anyone about the baby."

"You can trust Robin. She's like a lawyer or a doctor—professional privilege. Plus, her husband is the law."

Jodie sighed. "I'll talk to Robin, but I'm sure we have plenty of time."

"I hope you're right. I want everything to go smoothly." They walked out of the shadows of the bridge into the late winter sunshine.

"I come from a long line of very healthy women who deliver babies with no problems. I'll be fine."

Travis pushed aside his doubts as the sun filtered down through the canopy of trees and fell on Jodie's blond hair. "Tell me more about this family of Amazons," he said as he took her hand and once more started walking.

THE AFTERNOON in San Antonio passed quickly as they talked about their families and soon it was time for dinner. Travis knew a good Tex-Mex restaurant and suggested they stop there on the way back to Ranger Springs.

"Fine with me," Jodie said. "I love Mexican food."

Travis ordered a light beer and Jodie tried one of the nonalcoholic brews. After a few sips with her nachos, she pushed it aside.

"It just doesn't taste the same," she said. Travis ordered her a virgin margarita.

She sipped it, but didn't finish it, either. "It's not the same without tequila," she told him.

Finally the waitress brought her some iced tea. By then their fajitas had been served and they began to eat their dinner.

But later, just when Travis was thinking they might have a very enjoyable evening, Jodie said she wasn't feeling well.

"I don't think nonalcoholic beer and margaritas mix well with Tex-Mex food," she complained on the drive home.

"I'm sorry you're not feeling well."

Jodie rubbed her stomach. "I think I'm going to add a sensitive digestive system to my list of pregnancy complaints."

"Is the list really that long?"

"No!" She reached over and squeezed his hand. "Some heartburn and the need for afternoon naps is a small price to pay for a baby, right?"

Travis hoped she felt the same when her pregnancy started to show—and slowed down her career.

"THAT WASN'T SO BAD," Jodie said to Travis as they waved goodbye to the reporters. Neil was going to answer any lingering questions, then join them for lunch at the Four Square Café.

"Not too bad," Travis agreed. "I wouldn't want to do it all the time, though."

"I'm not really a celebrity. I'm pretty sure we won't be bothered again. It's a slow news time and a surprise wedding is always fodder for some papers and magazines."

"The photos of the wedding your guy from New York took turned out well," he said.

"Yes, they did. I'm having some made and framed of my mother and sister. Those were really good, also." Jodie decided that she'd get some of the wedding photos framed for his mother, father and sister as a surprise, since his family hadn't been able to come to the ceremony.

"Your mother is nice," he said. "I'm glad I got to meet her."

"And my sister?"

"Like I mentioned, she's different. Much more… well, not nearly as serious or career-oriented as you and your mother." He looked away, off into the distance…or the past. "My mother was career-oriented, also. She resented her family for taking her away from success."

"It's easy to blame someone else when things don't work out like we expect them to."

"True." He stopped on the covered sidewalk and faced her, then shook his head as if to clear his thoughts. "Jodie, you don't think you'll ever resent our baby for interfering with your career, do you?"

"No! Besides, the baby isn't keeping me from anything. This is the twenty-first century," she said, feeling as though Travis needed teasing. "I can have it all." She tugged him toward the café. Travis was just too conservative.

"I hope you're right."

Although she was sure Travis wasn't always overbearing, she could tell he liked to be in charge. He had confidence that he knew what was best and took action to force his agenda. That was fine in business, but it could make a marriage a bit difficult.

The bell over the door tinkled gaily, announcing their arrival at the café. The quaint restaurant was busy with the lunch crowd, including many of the people Jodie had met last week. The smell of fried, grilled and baked food filled the air. Charlene Jacks approached them with two menus.

"Hello! How are our newest newlyweds today?"

"Just fine, Charlene," Travis said. "We've been talking to those reporters who wanted the dish on our wedding."

Charlene chuckled. "They've been good for business. First we had a little betting pool going on what they wanted, but Thelma set us straight on that. Then we wondered if the two of you were going to cooperate."

"Jodie said the best way to get rid of them was to accommodate them, and she was right."

"Every time Alexi, Kerry and little Alex come to visit, we get a few of those European paparazzi. They're worse than the American press."

Fortunately, Jodie thought, they hadn't been following her the weekend she'd met Travis in Monte Carlo. If they'd been peeking into the room, they would have gotten a lensful of adults-only photos. The memories brought a warm flush to her skin.

"Is this booth okay?" Charlene asked, placing their menus down on a Formica-topped table in the back corner. With no one sitting next to them, they'd be able to talk in private.

"Fine. Jodie's publicist is going to be joining us. You might remember Neil," Travis said, sliding into the red vinyl seat, as if he knew Charlene would remember the rather flamboyant L.A. man.

Charlene raised her eyebrows. "Oh, yes. I'll show him back as soon as he gets here. In the meantime, do you want iced tea? Coffee?"

"Do you have some herbal tea?" Jodie asked. She didn't want to drink too much caffeine while she was pregnant. Despite the bright sunshine and moderate temperatures, the wind had a bit of a chill and hot tea would be good.

Her cheeks were probably pink and her hair windblown. She hoped that translated well in the photos taken today, since she knew she could just as easily look ruddy and stringy. Every time an unflattering photo of her appeared in the press, she felt her value as a model and a spokesperson decrease.

"I'll bring you some tea bags and a pot of hot water," Charlene said.

"When are you going to quit waiting tables?" Travis asked. He turned to Jodie. "Despite having two daughters married to millionaires, she won't stop working here at the café."

"Well, I have changed my job a little, Travis. I haven't let many people know, but my two daughters got together and bought the café for me as a fiftieth birthday present. I'm not just the most senior employee anymore, I'm the boss."

"Congratulations, Charlene. I know you love the place."

"I do. I can't see myself sitting around doing nothing, even though both girls have offered to support me if I wanted to retire early. But heck, I'm too young to retire."

"Of course you are," Travis agreed.

"I'll get your hot tea, Jodie, and your iced tea, Travis," she said, then walked into the back.

"You really are happy for her, aren't you?" Jodie asked. Travis had that kind of pleasant, contemplative look he sometimes wore when talking to or about his friends and neighbors.

"Of course. Charlene is a very nice lady. She had a tough life when the girls were young, I've been told, but all three of her daughters turned out well."

"I'm sure they did." Jodie leaned forward. "Thank you again for posing with me and talking to the reporters. I know that's not what you like, but you did a wonderful job."

"Thanks. It wasn't nearly as bad as I'd imagined."

"They weren't out for blood, or even real gossip. You can usually tell because if they're going to ambush you, they start pulling out 'facts' and 'quotes' that you've never heard before."

"I'll try to remember that, although I hope I won't be in that situation often."

Charlene returned with their drinks then left to serve another customer.

Jodie chose a tea bag and started brewing a lemon and mint flavor.

"Jodie, something's been bothering me, and since we are married, I thought I should bring it up."

"What is it?"

"While you were gone to California, I wondered why you didn't suggest I go with you. Was it because we argued about your plans to return for the meetings or was there another reason?"

Chapter Twelve

Jodie bobbed her tea bag in water and tried to remember if she'd even considered inviting Travis to come with her. She hadn't. She shook her head. "I'm obviously not very good at being married. Honestly, it never crossed my mind that you'd want to come to L.A. with me."

"To tell you the truth, I didn't think of it, either, until you were already gone."

"But when you did, it made you angry?"

"No, not angry. More like…disappointed."

"Then I suppose there's hope for us yet, because if we want to be together, that's half the battle."

Travis smiled. "Oh, I want to be together with you. If you'd like, I can show you just how much later."

Jodie felt her skin heat and her breath catch. Just as she was thinking about snuggling into his bed, the bell over the door tinkled again. Neil bustled through the restaurant, making a beeline for their booth.

Neil sat beside Travis, his eyes alight. "You totally impressed them, Jodie. Oh, and you, too, Travis. They think you are the most ideal newlyweds since…hmm, no, they didn't stay married. Oh, well, it doesn't matter," he said with a wave of his hand. "I'm sure the articles will be flattering. Of course they want more, but I explained that they need to respect your privacy for now, since you're on your honeymoon."

"Yes, we are," she replied neutrally, thinking of the fiasco of the trip to the cabin and the time they'd spent apart while she was in California.

"I hope we don't have to do this often," Travis said.

"You won't. The press just thinks it's romantic, the way you were introduced by royalty in Europe and then ran off and got married a month later."

"We didn't run off," Travis protested.

"Just a term of speech," Neil explained. "And speaking of running off, I need to get back to Austin to catch my flight to L.A. I have a meeting tomorrow with that sixteen-year-old swimsuit sensation and her mother. Such a stage mother," he said dramatically.

"I'm sure you'll do a fine job for them."

"I'll see you next week when you're in L.A. for the second round of meetings, right?"

"Right."

Charlene came up to their table. "Can I get you something to drink?" she asked Neil. "And I'll take your lunch orders whenever you're ready."

Neil requested a triple skinny latte, at which point Charlene looked at him as though he were crazy. "We have regular or decaf coffee."

"Regular," he answered with a sigh. When Charlene

left, he rolled his eyes. "This town is so far behind the times."

Jodie felt embarrassed. Just yesterday she'd told Travis that Ranger Springs needed a Starbucks. Now here was Neil, expressing the same sentiment, only not quite as kindly. "They have very good coffee. And it's not overpriced, either."

"Well, that's hardly the point. If a person wants a latte, they should be able to have one."

Travis scoffed, but didn't say anything.

"I don't remember 'life, liberty, latte and the pursuit of happiness' in the Declaration of Independence," Jodie answered.

"Don't tell me you're getting used to a small town. You, who doesn't even like the 'burbs?"

"This town has a lot to offer. Nice people, a safe community and a clean environment."

"Why, you're becoming a country girl!"

"Give me a break, Neil! I just got married." She glanced at Travis and saw his slight smile.

"I think Jodie is a country girl at heart. She's all-American. She's the 'girl next door,' according to the cosmetics company."

"She's a California girl with a very bright future for the next few years."

Travis frowned. "What do you mean, a few years?"

"She's a model and a cosmetics spokesperson. How many over-forty cosmetics contracts do you think are granted? Not many, I'll tell you. Jodie is smart to strike while the iron is hot, so to speak."

"Neil is right. I won't have this career forever."

"You can do whatever you want," Travis claimed, but Jodie knew it wasn't that easy. Her career in front of the cameras was limited to maybe another ten years, if she took care of herself. Before long, she needed to decide what else she wanted to do. Perhaps her own line of clothes or cosmetics, or both. Or perhaps something behind the cameras, finding and developing new talent.

Charlene brought Neil's coffee and took their orders—a club sandwich and chips for her, cheeseburger and fries for Travis. When Neil excused himself to wash his hands, Travis turned to Jodie.

"We never did finalize plans to move your things to my house. Do you think you'll have time to arrange that when you go back to L.A. next week?"

"I—I'm not sure what my schedule will be. I'll have to look at my planner."

"Do you have a lot of furniture?"

"Not a large amount. Enough to fill a two-bedroom, twelve-hundred-square-foot condo. Most of it wouldn't go in your house, though. It's pretty modern. My home in Newport Beach has lots of white walls, huge windows and stainless steel in the kitchen."

Travis nodded. "We can put whatever you'd like above the garage. I finished out the space for an apartment, but never did furnish it."

Jodie felt like squirming under his scrutiny. He wanted her to tell him that she'd pack up everything right away and move to Texas. That she'd just travel when she absolutely had to, and make Ranger Springs her new home. But she didn't feel that way, despite her defense of this small town. Her condo *was* home while she was in L.A.

And Travis still called the ranch "his house." Not "their house." How could she give up everything she loved in California to move in with a man who didn't think of them as a couple, even though she wanted him to understand?

If she argued with Travis about this, however, he would get angry again and then they'd never make progress on their marriage. The best thing was to keep quiet about her feelings without out-and-out lying to him.

"I'll work something out," she told him finally. She'd keep her condo…for now. She planned to make their marriage work, but she would also have a Plan B.

TRAVIS LIT A FIRE in the wide hearth in the great room. There was a chill in the air outside, but inside, it was warm. He and Jodie had spent yesterday and today together without getting into an argument.

Even the photos and interviews with the reporters in town hadn't been that bad. Neil had paved the way and Jodie had taken the lead in talking to them. He'd been able to play the role of the doting, noncelebrity husband. He was glad to stay out of the spotlight. As an architect he was well respected and he didn't need the additional publicity. He turned down jobs all the time because of previous commitments or because he wasn't interested in the client, property or function of the building.

With the wedding, interviews and travel out of the

way for now, perhaps he and Jodie could once again focus on their marriage. He'd been encouraged when she'd defended his hometown, telling Neil the attributes of small-town living. Before that, he wasn't even sure she liked Texas.

"Mmm, the fire smells good," she said, strolling into the room in a pair of comfortable baby-blue sweats and bulky socks. She'd brushed out her shoulder-length hair and scrubbed her face. She'd probably done more than just washed off her makeup, but he really had no idea what her nightly routine was. It probably involved lots of those mysterious potions that women used in almost ritualistic sequences. He'd observed the behavior in both his ex-wife and his sister.

"I made us some hot chocolate," he said.

"Sounds great. I hope you used lots of fattening ingredients. I've lost two pounds since we got married, and that's not good."

"If you lose weight that easily, why not let yourself level off?"

"Because my natural body size is probably a twelve, but that's too big for regular modeling and too small for plus size. I need to keep my weight up, but at the same time, exercise quite a bit so I don't get flabby."

Jodie certainly wasn't flabby. She was well-endowed and substantial, soft where a woman should be soft, but her muscles were toned. He couldn't imagine that anyone would say she was fat. He liked the way Jodie looked and felt.

He took a seat on the couch facing the fire and she

joined him there, picking up her mug of cocoa and leaning back against the pillows.

"Thanks for letting me use your office. I'd forgotten to fax my initialed copy of the contract. Felicia handled some last-minute changes."

"No problem. Use whatever you'd like, whenever you need to. I do most of my work in my studio, so the home office is usually available." He took a sip of hot chocolate, watching Jodie over the rim. "Was that the cosmetics company contract?"

"Yes. We had to tweak the no-compete clause just slightly because of some of the modeling assignments."

"I hope they're going to work with you on your schedule once they learn you're pregnant."

"I'm sure they will. As a matter of fact, they might want to play it up. We may have to do some more interviews as a couple."

"That's fine, but mostly I was concerned about your health. I hope they're considerate of the fact that traveling will become more inconvenient for you…later."

"That's very sweet of you to be concerned," she said, smiling at him. "Most people I know are concerned that I work more, not less."

He rubbed some strands of her hair between his fingers. "I want you to be happy, Jodie, and I want our baby to be healthy."

"I know. That's why it's so sweet. I burst into your life, but you've taken everything so well, even when I made you angry."

"I didn't mean to get angry. I suppose I had such unrealistic expectations for how things would be once we got married. I focused on getting through the ceremony, but I now understand that it takes more to make a marriage than saying vows in front of witnesses. It takes communication, and that's what we're working on, right?"

"Right," she said with a drowsy smile. She rested her cheek against his hand, which made him feel all warm and protective inside. Or maybe it was the fire and the hot chocolate, but he didn't think so. Jodie was changing him in ways he hadn't imagined two weeks ago.

"You are so beautiful," he said softly, watching her smile again.

"I don't have on a speck of makeup."

"You don't need any to make you pretty. I think that cosmetics company knows that, which is why they picked you. You're going to make them look good no matter what."

"That's so nice. You make me want to cry."

"Don't cry."

"Sometimes I can't help it. My hormones are going crazy. I feel so emotional at times. Other times I just want to sleep for a week."

"I think tonight you want both—a good cry and a long night's sleep."

"Maybe," she said, smothering a yawn. "But maybe that's not all I want." She turned to look at him with luminous eyes and a sultry smile. His heart skipped a beat and emotion surged through him, warming him more than the fire. When he kissed her, she tasted of chocolate and a promise of passion. But there was a hint of more, a glimpse of forever, that left him shaken. He didn't want all those soft emotions, even as he embraced the passion. He wanted a solid marriage, a happy wife and healthy baby. He'd never mentioned love, yet that seemed to be what Jodie silently offered. He didn't want love…but he desperately wanted Jodie right now.

They made love in front of the fireplace. She urged him on, her hunger a tangible force in the quiet house. With effort he kept himself in check, bringing them both to pleasure. She might be disappointed that he wasn't the wild and innovative lover he'd been in Monte Carlo, but he would never hurt Jodie or their baby.

At the same time, he wasn't willing to let himself be hurt by falling in love. Respect and passion—those were enough.

GWENDOLYN CALLED the next morning as Jodie was sipping her one and only cup of real coffee. Despite her unease when she recalled Travis's unusual restraint, which made her try even harder to unleash the passion she knew he was capable of giving, she'd slept well and felt ready to take on the world.

She felt like taking Travis back to bed with her.

"Hi, Gwendolyn. What's up?"

"I meant to tell you this last night. We've started an exercise class at the community center. I know you're probably accustomed to a fancy gym, but if you'd like to join us, you might find it fun."

"That sounds great. When is the class?"

"At ten o'clock each morning. I'm going over soon. We always have a nice turnout. You could meet some of the other ladies from town."

"Wonderful. I'll get directions from Travis and see you there."

She hung up the phone and turned to her husband. "I'm going to exercise with Gwendolyn. There's a class at the community center."

He frowned. "Are you sure you're supposed to do that when you're pregnant?"

"My doctor said I could continue doing anything that I normally do, as long as I don't overexert myself. I don't think an exercise class here will be very strenuous. Not like a hot spinning class at the gym in L.A."

"Hot spinning?"

"High-speed stationary biking in a superheated room. Not that I would usually take that class."

Travis grimaced. "Still—"

"I'll be fine, Travis. Don't worry about me. I'm as healthy as a horse, remember?"

"Even the best horse can founder or go lame," he said with a frown.

"Not me," she said, rinsing out her coffee cup and placing it in the sink. "Exercise is good for me."

Chapter Thirteen

Jodie had a great time at the community center exercise class. Gwendolyn had introduced her to a few women she hadn't met yet, and she saw several ladies she remembered from the Four Square Café and the wedding two weeks ago.

"Come by when you need your highlights touched up," Joyce Wheatley advised. "I know you're used to one of those fancy salons in the city, but I can do the same thing right here in your new hometown."

Jodie still felt a jolt of surprise when people referred to her moving to Ranger Springs, but she didn't correct them. She still didn't know how she felt about moving here. Travis's house was nice, but it wasn't yet home. And, darn it, she didn't know what would make the house a home. That wasn't her area of expertise.

"I'll make an appointment with you, Joyce. I'm sure you'll do a wonderful job." And if she didn't, Jodie could always have her stylist in L.A. fix the color. She didn't want to hurt the older lady's feelings, and to be honest, Joyce did a lovely job on her own hair, which was a natural-looking strawberry-blond.

After the class, they walked to the café for lunch. Jodie really enjoyed Gwendolyn's company. The English lady didn't know it yet, but they shared being pregnant. Jodie was slightly less than two months, while Gwendolyn was about four months along. It wouldn't be long now, however, before everyone knew her secret.

"I'm going to stop by Robin Parker's store for something Travis asked me to do. I'll see you the day after tomorrow, if you're going to be at class."

"I certainly will. I'm dedicated to having a very healthy baby and not embarrassing myself by being a total 'greenhorn' when it comes to delivery."

"Don't tell me Hank is putting pressure on you to become one of those natural childbirth, frontier women who has a baby and then goes out and plows the north forty!"

Gwendolyn laughed. "Not quite that horrid, I'm glad to say, but he's thrown out a few hints about how hardy Texas women are. We'll just see about that!"

"Good attitude. I'll see you soon."

Jodie walked to the corner, then crossed the street. Robin's store was in the middle of the block, which also faced the town square. She imagined the view in the spring and summer would be wonderful with all the trees and, no doubt, annual and perennial flowers.

The smell of potpourri and candles mixed with furniture oil to form a powerful scent as Jodie entered the store. The antique cash register was located in what appeared to be a counter from an old movie theater. As she looked around, she realized this *was* an old theater. Robin had done a fantastic job using the old space. Above, in what had been the balcony, were two bed-and-breakfast rooms. Neil had stayed here twice, but Jodie had never had time to come downtown to see the B and B.

"Jodie, how nice to see you."

"Thanks. Your shop is lovely. Travis has said such nice things about the place that I wanted to stop by."

"Travis is a sweetie. He's always throwing some business my way."

"This time he'd like to hire you for some help at his house. Er, our house. I'm still trying to get used to being married."

"No wonder, since you've been married about two weeks now, right?"

"Right." Jodie felt like squirming. Married two weeks and already they needed a nursery? Could she trust Robin with her secret?

"What do you need help with?"

"We want to redecorate one of the guest rooms."

"Oh? I thought Travis was finished with his decorating."

"Well, he was. We're changing the function of one of the rooms."

"Function? You mean like a study or a media room?"

"Not exactly." Jodie sighed. "Can you keep a secret? Decorator's confidence, sort of like a doctor or a lawyer?"

"Of course. My husband is chief of police. If I started blabbing everything I know, I'd be in big trouble."

Jodie glanced around to make sure no other customers lurked behind shelves. "We need one of the rooms as a nursery…but no hurry."

"Oh, Jodie, how great. You're going to start a family right away."

She grimaced and placed her hand on her stomach. "Actually, we got a little jump on the family. But we don't want anyone else to know yet, since we just got married. It's private, and besides, it wouldn't be good for my career."

"Oh, I understand. I won't tell anyone." She smiled and leaned closer. "And if anyone sees me with baby colors or patterns, I'll just say they're for me."

"You, too?"

"Three months and counting," she said, also placing a hand on her tummy. Jodie could barely tell, but there was a slight bulge in her khaki slacks.

"Congratulations!"

"You, me, Carole Rafferty and Gwendolyn McCauley. There must be something in the water around here," Robin said with a chuckle.

"In Monte Carlo, too," Jodie said with a smile. Both of them laughed and Jodie felt a camaraderie building between herself and the eclectic group of women who now called Ranger Springs home.

"How far along are you?"

"A little less than two months."

"Any morning sickness?"

"None, although I've had a little heartburn or upset

stomach after a few dinners. I've also developed a sudden need for naps."

"Oh, I know what you mean."

"While I'm here, do you have a rest room I could use? I drank so much water after exercise class."

"Sure. Just around the corner at the end of the counter."

Jodie smiled again at Robin, then hurried off to the rest room. She'd heard that pregnant women felt sudden urges to urinate, but so far she hadn't experienced that yet. This was the garden variety, too-much-to-drink need.

The rest room was decorated in red velvet and old movie posters, which was very fitting for the era in which the theater had probably been built. The stalls had been given a black, gray and white faux marble finish to match the countertop. Robin certainly did have a flare for design.

She'd done it! She'd started the nursery decorating process—even though they wouldn't need the room for many months. Travis had calmed down, the reporters were satisfied, her career was still on track and she had time to make a decision about the condo in Newport Beach.

But when she pulled up her oversize T-shirt and wiggled out of her spandex pants, she felt her world come crashing down.

"TRAVIS, NOW DON'T PANIC, but you need to meet us at the Wheatley Clinic."

"Robin? What are you talking about?"

"Jodie came to see me after exercise class and—"

"Jodie? Is she all right?"

"I think so, Travis, but there's a little problem."

"How little?"

"Travis, dammit, just get to the clinic. I don't know the details and you need to be here with your wife."

She disconnected the call before he could ask more questions, before he could collect his thoughts. *Jodie.* Something was wrong with Jodie...or the baby.

His baby.

He leaped from his drafting stool and ran down the hallway. His keys! Where had he put them? Racing past the breakfast counter, he spotted them lying beside his cell phone. He grabbed everything and raced outside.

Robin was already at the clinic with Jodie. Everything was going to be fine. Amy Phillips was a good doctor. She'd know what to do...for whatever was wrong, he thought as he turned the key and floored the gas.

He drove way too fast around the town square, risking a ticket or worse. He knew it, but he couldn't seem to slow down. He had to get there quickly, before something happened. Something that would change his well-balanced life.

Jodie had forced him to marry her in a way, but she'd also forced him to stop living on the sidelines. He cared for her and for their tiny little baby.

Please, God, not the baby. Not the precious little life they'd created together. He shouldn't have made love to Jodie last night, when she was already tired. He'd tried very hard to be careful, but what if even "normal" activity was too much?

He slid to a stop in front of the clinic, threw the SUV into park, turned off the engine and raced inside.

Everything looked so calm and normal. And quiet. He could hear his raspy breathing and pounding heart as he smelled the antiseptic scent of the medical offices.

Gladys looked up from the receptionist desk. "Travis, you need to calm down. You're going to hyperventilate."

"Where is she, Gladys? What's wrong with Jodie?"

"She's in Exam One with Dr. Amy. Now you calm yourself before you go into that room, Travis. You're going to scare her to death if you go in there all wild-eyed."

Scare her? He was the one who was frightened out of his mind. And he supposed his eyes were wild, since that's how he felt ever since Robin's words had penetrated his work-induced fog.

"Okay, Gladys, but is she okay? Robin wouldn't tell me what's wrong."

"I'm sure Jodie's going to be fine. She's relaxing and talking to the doctor. You don't need to give her another scare."

"Another scare? What was the first one?"

"Deep breaths, Travis. Then you can go in and see her."

Calm down fast, he told himself as he gasped a lungful of air. If something was terribly wrong, Gladys wouldn't be so calm. There would be screaming or yelling or some sound coming from Exam One. Within a minute, which seemed like twenty, he felt himself gaining control.

"You can go on in," Gladys said, "but be calm. Be positive. Don't start pelting her with questions. Remember that a husband should be supportive. This isn't a problem you can solve."

"Okay, supportive." Gladys was right—his first instinct was to find out what was wrong and to fix it, he thought as he walked down the short hall to the first room on the right. He took another deep breath and opened the door.

Jodie lay flat on the exam table, her knees bent and feet flat on the padded surface. She wore one of those pastel-printed cotton gowns and she looked pale and tense.

"Jodie," he breathed.

She smiled and held out her hand, which he grasped and held on tight. "I'm glad Robin got in touch with you."

He felt like taking her in his arms and demanding to know what had happened. Instead he asked as calmly as possible, "How are you?"

"I'm doing okay. False alarm, Dr. Amy said."

"False alarm for what?" he asked.

"Jodie suffered a broken blood vessel that made her think she had a far more serious problem."

"Broken blood vessel? That sounds serious."

"Not really. It probably happened during exercise class. It's common in pregnant women, who have increased blood flow to the uterus."

"The baby…" He couldn't finish the sentence.

"There's no indication that there's a problem. We're going to do a sonogram, though, to make sure. You got here just in time."

"Travis?"

"Yes, sweetheart?"

She squeezed his hand. "I'm glad you're here."

He smiled at his wife. *His wife.* Until this moment, he'd felt like a nervous suitor, then a frustrated bridegroom, then a real bridegroom, but not really a husband. "I'm glad I'm here, too, but I wish you hadn't scared ten years off my life."

"I'm sorry." She tried to slip her hand out of his grip.

"I'm not blaming you. I didn't mean that." Why did he always mess up around Jodie? "I was so surprised when Robin called. I thought maybe Dr. Amy was going to have to treat me for hyperventilation."

Jodie smiled. "I wish we could have told you something on the phone, but neither Robin nor I knew what was happening at first."

"I understand. You didn't find anything wrong, right?" He looked at the doctor.

"No, it probably won't happen again. Just to be safe, though, take it easy for a few days. No hard exercising or horseback riding. No sex, either."

"Of course not," he said quickly. The last thing he wanted to do was to hurt Jodie or their baby. He wondered again if any of their activity—even though he'd done his best to be gentle—had brought on this problem. When they made love again, he'd be even more cautious and restrained. Which Jodie probably wouldn't appreciate…

"Okay, Jodie, I need you to lie flat and be still. The gel will be cold, but only for a moment."

Amy wheeled the sonogram machine closer, then draped a sheet across Jodie's thighs and lower abdomen.

She folded the gown back to reveal the soft, slightly tanned skin of Jodie's stomach.

"I guess our secret is out now," she said softly, watching the doctor. "I've already told Robin, too."

"It was going to be obvious soon anyway."

"Not for a couple of months."

"The news is safe with me and Gladys," Amy said, "and I'm sure Robin won't tell anyone. I don't think you have to worry. You can keep your secret for a while longer."

She worked in silence until an image began to develop on the screen. Travis couldn't tell what it was until the doctor pointed out the tiny little peanut-shaped blip.

"There's the baby," she said. "Still nice and secure inside of mom."

"Mom," he said with a smile. "How does that sound?"

"Scary," Jodie whispered. Still, she looked with awe at the image. "The pregnancy hadn't seemed completely real until today."

"I understand," Dr. Amy said. "That's perfectly normal. The first sonogram is usually done a little later except in a high-risk pregnancy. Since you don't have a family history of any problems and you're in excellent shape, we wouldn't have done one for another month or so. But now you have your first picture of the little one."

"You can make a still photo?" Travis asked.

"Yes. You can take it to the café and show everyone you're going to be a daddy."

"I might just have to wait awhile, until Jodie gives me the okay."

"Daddy," Jodie said with a bigger smile as she looked at the monitor. "How does *that* sound?"

He spoke past the lump in his throat. He realized that for years he'd never allowed himself to consider fathering a child. Maybe because he'd never found the right woman. Maybe because he hadn't dared to dream of a real family. "Sounds wonderful." He leaned down and kissed her lips. "Thank you for making me a father."

She looked up at him with something akin to love in her eyes. "You're welcome. I couldn't have done it without you."

WHEN TRAVIS ESCORTED HER out of the medical clinic after many thanks to Dr. Amy and Gladys, Jodie stopped and stared at the crazy way he'd parked the SUV. He was half on and half off the pavement, and there were skid marks on the dry winter grass.

He really had been upset. He really cared about her…and the baby.

She smiled to herself and clutched the photo close to her chest. Her baby. Their baby. She felt almost giddy.

"You look awfully good for a woman who nearly made me pass out from fright."

"I feel good for someone who just about made herself pass out from fright."

Travis drove her home much more sedately than he'd driven to the clinic. "Do you need anything on the way home? Food or medicine? Any cravings?"

"No, I'm fine. I had just eaten lunch with Gwendolyn before I went to Robin's Nest to talk to her about decorating the baby's room. That's when I discovered the blood. I screamed for Robin and she knew exactly what to do."

"We'll have to do something really nice to thank her."

"She's great. Everyone's been great."

"This is a nice town," Travis stated.

"Just like you told Neil yesterday."

"When I heard him order the latte, it reminded me of the remark I'd made in San Antonio, and I felt bad about saying that."

"You didn't mean anything by it. It's not unreasonable to want a Starbucks or a McDonald's or any other establishment that makes you feel at home. It's only unreasonable when you think it's your right to have a certain establishment, as though the world owes it to you to provide everything you're used to, all the time."

"That's very philosophical."

"Hey, I'm a deep guy."

"Really? I'll have to explore your depths later, when my mind is a little sharper. All I can think of now is going back to the ranch, sinking into a bed and sleeping for a day or two. After a nice warm shower, of course."

"Sounds good. I can arrange that."

"You're a good man, Travis Whitaker."

They drove in silence the rest of the way to the ranch, which was on the other side of town from the clinic. Jodie felt herself grow sleepy in the warm interior of the SUV. The adrenaline from her scare evaporated from her system like the morning sea mist over the Pacific coastline.

She vaguely noticed that they'd pulled into the garage. Travis turned off the car, and the quiet lulled her even more deeply into sleep. She knew she should get up, but she was so tired. She managed to unhook her seat belt, but couldn't muster the strength to open the door.

The interior light made her blink as strong arms wrapped around her. "Hang on tight, sweetheart," Travis said softly in her ear.

"You can't carry me," she protested.

"Sure I can. I'm a big guy."

"I'm a big girl," she said, laying her head on his shoulder.

"Yes, you are, but not too big for me. In fact, you're just the right size."

She felt herself being lifted out of the SUV and held on tight, just as he'd instructed. She hadn't been carried since she was a small child. Her mother used to carry her into their house when she'd gone to sleep in the back seat after they'd visited friends or gone out to dinner. She'd held her tight, making Jodie feel safe and loved as her mother had carried her to bed.

Travis made her feel the same way. Safe. Cared for. Loved. Tears formed in her eyes as he carried her through the door.

"I can walk. I'm awake now."

"You just relax. Don't start wiggling."

"I never wiggle."

"I remember when you wiggled."

She smiled and kissed his neck.

"Oh, now you're getting frisky, when we can't do anything about it."

"I was just being affectionate."

"Save it for later, when you're all recovered."

"I'm going to get better fast."

"Good Lord, I hope so."

Jodie chuckled. She felt so good right now. She wished Travis could carry her forever, but he was already breathing hard as they went through the mudroom and kitchen.

She opened her eyes when he walked past the stairs to the bedrooms above. "Where are you taking me?"

"To bed. To my bed."

"Why?"

"Because I want you there. I want to take care of you, watch over you."

She should go to the guest room, since they couldn't be intimate for several days. She should tell him that she could take care of herself, that she wasn't sick or even feeling bad anymore.

But she didn't. She let him carry her into his room and lay her on the bed.

"I told you I could carry you to bed," he said.

"Yes, you did. And the jury's still out on your back."

He chuckled. "My back is fine. Okay, I'm breathing a little harder than usual, but that doesn't mean anything. I get a little winded if I unload a bunch of fifty-pound feed sacks."

"Hmm, another good comparison. I'm as heavy as a bunch of fifty-pound feed sacks and as substantial as a house. You do know how to sweet-talk a girl, Travis Whitaker."

"You just wait, Mrs. Whitaker. As soon as you're well, I'll show you sweet talk."

"You just wait until I'm well, Mr. Whitaker. I'll climb into your bed on my own."

"Now that's something to take my breath away."

Chapter Fourteen

Jodie reclined against the pillows and decided that letting someone take care of her was pretty nice. She wouldn't want or expect this type of treatment forever, but for now, having breakfast in bed, complete with a folded newspaper and a single yellow rose—how'd he manage that?—was wonderful.

"Is Helen here?" she asked when he filled her cup with coffee.

"Yes, she's downstairs. I told her you weren't feeling well." Travis looked as handsome as usual, but a little drawn, as though he hadn't rested well. She had no idea how he'd slept because she'd taken a nap, awakened for dinner and fallen back to sleep again in his room, at his insistence. She had been aware that he'd lain on the other side of the bed. Close, but not touching her, probably out of concern for her condition.

Jodie selected a slice of toast. "This breakfast is great. I'm starving."

"How are you feeling?"

"Fine. Like nothing happened. I got up earlier and checked, and I seem to be okay today."

"That's good. I'm still worried, but not as much as yesterday."

"Don't worry, I'm as healthy—"

"As a horse. Yes, I remember your claims of Amazonian status. But just humor me for now. I've never had a pregnant wife before and I'm finding the reality a little scary."

"Poor Travis. I'll make it up to you, I promise."

That brought a grin to his face. "I'll hold you to that promise."

"You can hold me to all my promises." She grinned. "I promise."

They both laughed. As she ate, he sat on the bed and told her what he was working on and what he had to do later. She felt married this morning—waking up in his bed, eating breakfast…well, not together, but close.

"You know I have to go to California in a few days," she said tentatively. "I would suggest you go with me, but I'm going to be in a lot of meetings for a couple of days. They'll probably want me to do some voice and lighting tests to prepare for taping the commercials."

"Don't you think you should postpone your trip for a week or so? To make sure you're completely recovered."

"I'll be fine. Dr. Amy said I just needed to make sure I didn't have any more spotting."

"You need to take it easy."

"Look, I need to keep up with my obligations. I can't tell the cosmetics company that I'm just not feeling well. They expect me to be there. They're paying me a large amount of money to represent them."

A stubborn expression appeared on his face and he looked slightly angry. "You're going to have to tell them soon that you're pregnant."

"And I will, but not yet. I'm not quite two months."

"When?"

"I don't know. Probably at three months. Isn't that traditional? As long as I'm not disrupting their schedule, I'm not worried about it. And in another month, we'll have the commercials and print ads in production."

"Their schedule? What about your needs!"

"They've hired my face and figure, my personality, to represent their product. I have to give them what they've paid for. Besides, it's best for my career, too. I have to think about post-cosmetics contracts. The time to plan for the future is now."

"What about your future as a mother? As a wife? Is that in your master plan?"

"Of course. I'm planning my schedule so I'll be able to take off with the baby and spend time with you."

"How much time, Jodie? Because I distinctly remember mentioning that I wanted us to stay married for keeps if we got married, and you agreed. You promised. I don't consider this a real marriage if you're always gone."

"I'm not always gone. I've been here a lot."

"But you'll always be leaving, won't you? You've always got another place to be."

"I—I never agreed to give up my life."

"I thought you were moving here to Texas. Are you planning on that?"

"Well, of course I'll be living here."

"Full time, as in moving here?"

She didn't know what to say to his question. She wasn't going to lie to him, but she felt as though he was putting her in an untenable situation.

"Travis, I wish you wouldn't continue to put pressure on me to move out of my condo. I really enjoy staying there while I'm in L.A. It's a great escape, only a block from the beach with an ocean view. I love my condo."

"A lot more than you could love it here," he said flatly.

"That's not what I mean!"

"I don't know what you mean because you won't tell me what you're thinking. You won't tell where I fit into your plans. I'm not even sure *if* I fit into your plans."

"Why are you asking me to choose between you and my career?" she said, throwing up her hands.

"I never said that. I just want you to make a commitment to me. To us. To our baby."

"I have made a commitment. I married you and I am having this baby. Those are facts, Travis. Those are commitments."

"You live out of a suitcase while you're here, Jodie. You treat the house like it's a hotel, never leaving a thing out of place."

"That's because this is *your* house. They're *your* things!"

"Then bring your things here, Jodie. Fill up all the closets and drawers. Unpack your knickknacks and put them everywhere. Rearrange my kitchen until I don't know where my utensils are, where to find a clean glass. For God's sake, Jodie, move in! This is your house now, too."

She stood beside the wide window, soaking in the weak sunlight, clenching her fists to keep from shaking. "I do live out of suitcases, Travis. I've done it for years. And despite what you offer, this is *your* house. You designed it, you built it. You even refer to it as yours, not ours. If I'm not the kind of woman you want, I'm sorry, but I can't be any different than who I am. I'm a career woman. I can't even cook! And as for messing up your house, putting my knickknacks around, I can't. I just can't, because…because I don't have any knickknacks."

She turned and ran down the hall and up the stairs to the safety of the guest room.

She should have stayed here. She never should have slept in Travis's bed. He'd tempted her with how things could be. He'd made her believe that she could have it all.

But she couldn't. She couldn't have it all because she couldn't change who she was.

Travis didn't want the real Jodie. He wanted a myth. He wanted the girl next door, not the career woman with her own condo.

She flung herself down on the bed and cried for everything she'd never had.

TRAVIS RODE OUT to the spring, as he'd done over two weeks ago when Jodie had made her first offer of marriage. He needed to think. And unlike that other time, a sad type of anger ate at his insides. The walls of the house he'd carefully planned and built pressed down around him until he couldn't breath.

He urged his gelding into a gallop, across the hills and toward the line of trees. Hoofbeats pounded in rhythm to his heart as he approached the edge of his property where trees circled the springs and lined the fencerow. The live oaks and cedars remained green all winter, but the rest of the limbs were bare and twisting against the cloudy sky. He reined to a stop, taking in the edge of his property as his horse blew hard after their dash across the land. He swung down from his gelding, placed one booted foot on a rock, and knew it was time to look within himself.

Instead of the gently moving water in the natural pool, he saw Jodie's tear-streaked face and could hear the hurt in her voice as she told him she couldn't be the kind of woman he wanted.

Hell, he didn't want a certain kind of woman. He knew what he didn't want, though. A self-absorbed wife who lived only to satisfy her needs. He didn't think Jodie was such a career woman that she couldn't care about him or their child.

She just didn't feel married to him. She'd admitted that she hadn't felt pregnant until yesterday. And if they couldn't live as man and wife, in the same house and the same bed, how could they become a couple? How could they be equal parents to their child?

He wanted to be connected to Jodie through more than the baby. That was the reason they'd married, but he didn't want their child to be the reason they stayed together. He wanted more now that he'd gotten a glimpse, just a small peek, at what might be.

He didn't quite understand what had happened in his bedroom. Jodie claimed she lived out of suitcases, that she couldn't make his house a home. But how could that be true? She obviously thought of her condo as her home in California. She'd bought furniture and furnishing to make herself comfortable. Why couldn't she do the same thing here?

He wasn't sure what he'd done to make her feel unwelcome in his house. Obviously this was her house, too, legally and morally, since they were married. She'd said he referred to the house as his rather than theirs, but he couldn't remember doing that. Perhaps he had made some comment. If so, he hadn't meant anything by it. He'd certainly never considered that Jodie might be offended.

His sister had claimed that men were oblivious to the finer nuances of emotion, speech, body language and other communication that women understood. Perhaps that's what was going on between him and Jodie.

Some of his "good ol' boy" friends and neighbors would tell him that Jodie was just being too sensitive, but he didn't think so. She'd gotten a little more emotional because she was pregnant, although her condition didn't make her irrational. Maybe she was seeing something he'd never imagined, something he hadn't intended.

He needed to go back to the house, to talk to Jodie and to explain that he hadn't meant to push her away, to make her feel unwelcome. He didn't think less of

Jodie because she didn't collect things, cook or make a "nest" as some women did. She had other strengths, other abilities, that he admired.

He wanted to recapture the magic he'd experienced all too briefly with Jodie. He wanted to see that look in her eyes, the emotion she'd displayed yesterday at the clinic when they'd seen the sonogram of their baby.

With a renewed sense of purpose, Travis swung into the saddle and headed home. Not to his house, but to theirs.

But after he'd unsaddled and stabled his gelding and walked into the too quiet house, he knew something was wrong. He found Jodie's note lying on the breakfast bar and tore it open.

He read the note out loud. "'I've gone back early for my meetings. I'll be at my condo and will contact you later, after I've had time to think.'"

She'd signed it with a simple "J." Not even her whole name. Definitely no sentiment, not that he'd expected "love always" or even "best wishes." She'd just walked out without a word.

And then he saw the photo of their baby, their little "peanut," lying on the counter. He picked it up with trembling hands, remembering the emotion they'd both felt when Dr. Amy had produced the image on the sonogram. If he'd been cynical about Jodie, he would have said she was taunting him by leaving the photo. But he knew her better than that now. She'd left the picture because she knew the baby meant so much to him, too.

"Damn," he muttered. While she was taking action, he'd been thinking about their situation, mulling things over in private. And now she was on her way to the place she considered her home. To the place where she unpacked those suitcases she lived out of, where she watched the sun set over the Pacific and decorated—or not—to suit her own tastes. Not his, not anyone else's.

Could she ever think of Ranger Springs as her home?

JODIE'S FIRST PRIORITY was to find an excellent obstetrician in Los Angeles, then make an appointment to have her condition checked. Seeing the tiny life on the screen and feeling the fear that something was wrong had made her more committed than ever to having a safe pregnancy and a robust baby.

She'd flippantly proclaimed to Travis that she was as healthy as a horse and that no women in her family ever had problems with pregnancy, but she finally accepted that she wasn't invulnerable. She could have problems just like any other woman.

She'd never felt as connected with the women she represented—all the girls-next-door and big girls and ordinary women—than she did now that she had problems. A non-consequential medical problem, she hoped, and more important in the long run, a man problem.

She'd made a vow to herself that she would learn to be a wife, and she actually thought she'd been making progress, but then they'd had another argument and she'd walked—or run—away while Travis had been out riding.

Just as he'd run out on her when they'd argued before.

She probably shouldn't have done that, but darn it, she hadn't seen any reason to stay around there and be tense. To avoid each other, or worse still, to try to be polite when all she felt was hurt. She didn't know how to cope with these feelings, so she'd run back to California.

With a sigh she swung her luggage onto the bed and began to unpack. Regardless of what she'd told Travis, she didn't live out of a suitcase all the time. And she was beginning to think that perhaps she didn't want to travel so much. The idea of having a real home, a real family, had planted itself into her mind and was slowly growing.

She didn't have to model, either on the runway or in print ads, on a regular basis. She could be a cosmetics spokesperson and explore some of her other options. Designing clothing had a certain appeal, and who wouldn't love to have a fragrance named for them?

She was going to take these few days to rest, to get checked by the doctor and to think about what she really wanted. She also had to think about what was reasonable, given her sometimes volatile relationship with Travis. Could they make their marriage work if they couldn't communicate? The next move was up to her.

TRAVIS DIDN'T KNOW what to do. Take action, as every atom in his body screamed, or be patient, as he imagined his sister Kate would advise. One thing was certain—pacing the rooms of his house and wishing Jodie would magically appear wasn't getting him anywhere.

It was after two o'clock in the afternoon and she was no doubt already back in Los Angeles.

"Damn," he muttered again, grabbing the keys to the SUV. He needed to get out, to do something. And in times like this, he needed the council of his friends.

Hank might be a big kidder and appear to be a carefree cowboy, but he was smart and loyal. Besides, he'd learned a lot about women in the past two years since marrying Gwendolyn. Hank might know what to do, Travis thought as he quickly dialed his neighbor's home number.

"I'll buy you a beer and listen to your advice on how to fix my screwed-up life if you'll meet me at Shultze's Roadhouse," he said as soon as Hank answered.

"What did you do to make Jodie angry?"

"Hell, lots of things. Just meet me and I'll try to remember everything I did wrong."

"That may take a while. I'll tell Wendy not to wait supper for me."

They hung up and Travis kept driving. A nice, dark honky-tonk was where a man should go to solve his problems, right?

Schultze's Roadhouse sat right on the state highway, just outside the city limits but close enough that everyone came here for beers, burgers, barbecue and camaraderie. Two pool tables held court in the back room and the juke box featured only country-western music, except for a couple of Frank Sinatra classics that Olive, the bartender, listened to when she wanted to be maudlin.

Maybe he should listen to them today, Travis thought as he pulled into the parking lot, found a space near the front door and killed the engine. Or maybe not. He was already feeling pretty sorry for himself.

At midafternoon the place was pretty empty. A few die-hards sat at the end of the bar, kind of like the two regulars on "Cheers," only in overalls and gimmee caps. The pervasive smell of cigarette smoke hung in the air and coated every surface and a neon beer sign made an annoying buzzing noise as he walked up to the bar to order.

"Hey, Olive. Make mine a long-neck, and get Hank whatever he wants when he comes in. I'll be in the booth over there," Travis said, nodding toward the back corner where they'd have some privacy to talk.

"Sure enough, Travis."

Olive delivered his beer. Within another five minutes, Hank arrived, picked up his own beer and settled across from Travis in the booth.

"So, what's up with Jodie?"

"She's gone back to California."

"One of those trips you mentioned?"

"No, not really. One of those arguments I didn't mention."

"Ah," Hank said, then took a long draught of his beer. "You want to talk about what you did to screw up?"

"No, but it's the only thing I haven't tried yet, so listen up."

Chapter Fifteen

Jodie's schedule filled up quickly once the creative team knew she was back in California early. Fortunately, she'd located a good doctor who'd had a late-afternoon cancellation yesterday. She'd discovered that, just as Dr. Amy Phillips had told her, she was fine now. The broken blood vessel had healed completely.

She could resume all her normal activities, the doctor had said with a knowing smile. For Jodie, that meant work, work and more work. Not making love, as she and Travis had teased each other about a couple of days ago.

She sighed as she stepped out of her sporty little Audi convertible in the office building's parking garage. She had meetings most of today with ad execs, a corporate V.P., a still photographer, the video production crew and some of the creative team she'd met before. In addition, Neil would join them later in the day to coordinate press activities in preparation for the ad campaign.

"This is what you've dreamed of," she whispered to herself as she waited for the elevator. Too bad she kept thinking about Travis, the husband she'd run out on in Texas. And her precious and fragile baby. And sex. Don't forget the sex she wasn't having!

The elevator bell dinged, reminding her of the tiny cluster of bells on the door of the Four Square Café. Of all the nice people there who led much less hectic lives. With another sigh, she stepped into the brass-and-mirrored car that would take her thirty-six floors up to the world she'd chosen.

Seven hours later she emerged from the downtown building, said "Goodbye" to half the team and "See you tomorrow" to the rest, and claimed her car. She'd be driving home through rush-hour traffic, but she'd declined the offer of dinner and more talk of the cosmetics campaign. She'd claimed fatigue from her flight—plus she'd endured some jokes about her Texan keeping her up at night—as her excuse to get away from everyone. The truth was that she was bone tired because she hadn't gotten her daily nap, and all she wanted to do now was to curl up and watch the sun set over the Pacific from her second-floor balcony.

Normally she'd have a glass of wine beside her lounge chair, but that wasn't an option now. Not drinking wasn't a problem, but she realized she'd have to explain it to her friends and business associates. Pretty soon, she was going to have to tell them about the pregnancy anyway.

An hour and a half later, she pulled into her parking spot. All she wanted after she watched the sunset was a

long soak in the tub and about ten hours of uninter-
rupted sleep.

But when she saw the tall, handsome Texan silhouetted in the entrance hall to her building, her fatigue disappeared in an instant.

"TRAVIS."

He heard her breathe his name, producing the same
reaction as if she'd run her fingertips lightly up his
spine. She looked stylish in her black jumpsuit, which
zipped up the front and was cinched by a metal-stud-
ded leather belt. She also looked tired in her high-heeled
black sandals. "Hello, sweetheart."

Her large zebra-print purse slipped from her shoulder to the concrete walkway. A matching silk scarf
puddled on the concrete. "What are you... When did
you..."

He pushed away from the doorway and walked the
few feet separating them. "I would have come sooner,
but I just missed the earlier flight."

"Why?"

"Because I had a hellacious hangover this morning."

"No, I mean why did you come to L.A.?"

He stood in front of her and looked into her eyes. "A
married couple should be together during the tough
times. I want to be here for you, to make sure you're
healthy and safe and happy. To do whatever I can to
make your life easier and better. I can't do that when
I'm in Texas and you're in California, and I know you
need to be here for your career. It took me a while to

admit it, but I was being selfish. I wanted you in Texas with me."

"What happened?"

He shrugged. "When I realized that while I was out thinking about our relationship, you had taken action, I knew I needed to do the same thing. So I did what any red-blooded American male would do—I called up my best friend, met him at our local honky-tonk and drank way too many beers."

He saw a slight smile forming. "Did Hank tell you to fly out here and fetch me home?"

"No," Travis said, cupping her shoulders. "He told me that I needed to quit being so bossy and get myself out here to be with you. That's when I realized that where we were didn't matter as much as being together. I love the ranch, but I can be flexible. Why can't we have two homes?"

"Oh, Travis, are you serious? This isn't some duty thing, is it? You want to spend time out here with me?"

"Maybe not every time you need to have a meeting, but often. Occasionally I have to travel on business, and I'd love for you to come with me when you can. We have two careers and I hope we can both compromise."

"And what about the condo?"

"Well, I'm not sure yet since I haven't seen it inside." He grinned at her. "The outside doesn't look like something I'd design, but I think I might be able to live with that."

"Come inside and see."

"I thought you'd never ask."

She led him down the short walkway and up the stairs. "The view's better up here."

"I saw the ocean when I drove in. The waves are huge here in Newport Beach."

"You should see them when a storm is coming in. I can hear the roar from the ocean and feel the salt spray on my balcony, over a hundred yards from the beach."

"Sounds wonderful. I'd like to see that sometime."

She smiled as she unlocked the door. Apparently he'd said the right thing for a change.

"Make yourself comfortable. I'm going to fix us something cold to drink," she said as she slipped off her sandals and placed her large purse on a sleek leather chair.

He stood in the living room and looked around. Her place was a fairly generic modern structure with furniture and art consistent with the design. Bold splashes of color—red, yellow and purple—contrasted to the white walls, light wood floors and white leather sofa. The decorating gave him insight into the real Jodie Marsh, because this was her home, not her office or some other public place. This condo meant enough to her that she didn't want to give it up.

At the same time he noticed the lack of personal items. There were only a few artfully framed photos of her mother and sister and her. Over the stucco-covered fireplace was a very modern acrylic. Near the wide sliding-glass doors leading to the balcony were pedestals with beautiful, brightly colored hand-blown glass. They looked perfectly suitable for the condo, and just as impersonal for Jodie. They could have belonged to any-one, yet Jodie was absolutely unique.

She walked back into the room with tall, slender glasses of iced tea. "I think I remembered the way you like it sweetened."

"I'm sure it's fine," he said, taking the glass. "Does your mother live close by?"

"In Orange. That's in Orange County. In traffic it's about forty minutes," she answered before taking a long swallow of her drink.

"I'll bet you still have your room in her home."

The glass paused as she stopped drinking and looked at him curiously. "How did you know that?"

"Because I'll bet that's where all your knickknacks and mementos are kept. I'll bet you have a room there with remnants of your childhood. I'll bet that there are things in that room that explain your success, your phi-losophy of life and your personality."

"Everyone has things left over that they don't want to part with."

"Yes, they do, and they all tell a story. I think you made yourself into who you are today—a very success-ful, completely modern career woman. However, I don't think that's all there is to you. I think that there's another side of you that you've never really explored. I think it's stored away at your mother's home."

"Oh, you do? Have you become a psychologist in ad-dition to an architect?"

"No, I just find you fascinating."

"I'm not so complicated."

"I didn't say complicated. A person doesn't have to be complex to be fascinating."

"Hmm. I'll have to think about that."

"Think about this, too," he said, stepping closer. "Our marriage and our baby could be the part of you that's been stored away on your climb to personal success. If you'll let us into your world, I think we can make you complete."

She leaned her head against his shoulder. "I thought I was complete until I met you."

"I think it's hard to know when we're complete. I thought I was happy, too, until you showed me how empty my life was."

"Maybe we were meant to be together."

"Lord, I hope so," he whispered right before he tipped her chin up and kissed her.

JODIE SLANTED HER HEAD and leaned into his kiss, loving the feel of his lips on hers, his body pressed close. His tongue slipped inside and her heart skipped a beat, then began to pound in rhythm to his thrusts. Oh, this man could kiss.

He broke away to nibble his way down her jaw and neck to the collar of her jumpsuit. All she could do was close her eyes and tremble.

"I want you so much, Jodie," he said against that sensitive spot where her neck and shoulder joined, "but not unless you're okay. I don't want to hurt you."

"I went to the doctor yesterday afternoon," she said, her voice sounding breathless above the blood pounding in her veins. "I'm fine. The doctor said there was no reason we couldn't resume normal relations. I—I guess she meant normal for most people."

His magical lips stopped and he pulled back. "What do you mean by that?"

"When we made love that first weekend, it was never normal," she said as she continued unbuttoning his shirt. "Then after we got married, I missed the wildness, the passion. I wanted everything to be like it was in Monte Carlo and I resented you because you were so careful, so controlled."

"I did what I thought was right at the time. The idea of hurting you or the baby frightened me."

"I've told you I'm not some fragile china doll." She pulled his shirt apart and ran her hands from his abs to his pecs, then circled his neck.

"I know, but you drive me crazy," he murmured before he kissed her again. His hands molded her back, cupped her bottom and moved back up again, as though he were learning the shape of her for the first time. Then one hand eased between them and he edged that big silver zipper lower, until he reached her belt.

"I want you to be crazy."

"Only if you promise me that you'll tell me if I'm too rough. If anything I do is the least bit uncomfortable."

"I promise. Please, let yourself go. I want your passion, Travis. I want it more than anything."

He kissed her, pulling her close against his arousal, making her a little crazy herself. Then his hand sought her zipper, and she pulled away slightly. "This jumpsuit is completely wrong for a seduction," she said. It was also impractical for slipping in and out of the rest room while in meetings. She wouldn't be able to wear it when she was more pregnant and had to go more often.

"Oh, I don't know. I think it's pretty darn sexy. Are you sure you were in meetings all day?"

"Yes, I was in meetings. And, thank you. I didn't feel sexy until I saw my handsome, tall cowboy in the walkway."

"You know what would be even more sexy?"

She had a few ideas. "What?"

"If we both adjourn to your bedroom."

"Hmm," she said, taking his hand and guiding him down the short hallway, "you want to see the rest of the condo?"

"Later. Right now all I want to see is your bed. Then I want to watch you strip out of that jumpsuit."

"I think that can be arranged."

She moved to her entertainment armoire and flipped on the low-wattage lamp which cast a soft golden light over the room. Travis looked around quickly, taking in her streamlined but comfortable decor. Her bedroom was large, done in soothing neutrals and heavy drapery panels that he guessed kept the morning light out when she wanted to sleep late.

"Very nice," he said, grabbing one edge of her comforter and sweeping it from the bed. He slipped out of his shirt, unbuckled his belt and quickly stripped out of his boots and socks. "Now, about that jumpsuit…"

She smiled as he leaned back against the pillows. Her

zipper was already down to her waist, revealing her black lace bra and lots of cleavage. She stood at the end of the bed, her gaze locked with Travis's, and unbuckled the silver-studded black belt. She whipped it off, then flung it on the bed, where it looked rather naughty lying there on the white Egyptian cotton sheets.

"Nice accessory," Travis drawled, "but I'm not really into that sort of thing."

"Neither am I. At least, I've never tried it."

"Hmm," he said with a mysterious smile.

She eased the zipper lower, revealing the matching black lace panties and lots of skin. She shouldn't be nervous, she told herself, because Travis had seen all of her before. Several times. But now that they were married and she was carrying his child, she felt even more shy than she had in Monte Carlo.

"I think it's time to lose the jumpsuit," Travis said, his voice husky.

She slipped first one arm, then the other, from the sleeves, all the time watching her husband. He shifted on the bed, bringing her attention to the impressive bulge in his jeans. Her heart began to race as she remembered their days and nights together, and suddenly she wanted out of her clothes and into her bed.

She leaned down, giving him full view of her cleavage, and pushed the jumpsuit the rest of the way off. When she straightened, she gave Travis a smile as she walked toward the bed. "Your turn."

He rolled to the edge just as her knees touched the mattress. Placing his legs on either side of hers, he ran his hands from her waist around her back, bringing her closer. He nuzzled her breasts through her lacy bra, bringing her nipples to hard points.

She'd never been so grateful in her life for always wearing pretty, matching underwear.

He reached for the back catch on her bra, but she slid her hands to his hard biceps. "Not until you've lost the pants."

She made him stand and strip while she looked and admired and remembered. He excited her senses in every way—his looks, his scent, his words, his actions. She knew she'd never get tired of this man.

They sank to the bed together, and only then did she allow him to remove her underwear and drive her crazy with desire. She felt as if they hadn't made love for ages rather than weeks. She wanted him too much to go slow and gentle, but Travis wouldn't let her rush. He kissed her, driving her wild, but so slowly that she wanted to scream. And when he finally joined his body to hers, he gave her his passion, moving with strength and skill and the urgency she'd missed since they'd married.

She felt the familiar pressure building, then an urgency overtook her, the need to move against him with wild abandon. She chanted his name as she pressed upward, climbed upward, and finally broke through to the white-hot peak where only Travis could take her.

Before she could take a breath, he climaxed hard and long as she held him tight.

Minutes later she lay locked in his arms, her heart overflowing. She felt more than sexually satisfied, more than complete. She'd never felt this way before, and suddenly she realized why.

She'd fallen in love with her husband.

TRAVIS WOKE SOMETIME later to the sound of running water and the feel of a fresh breeze across his skin. His very naked skin. The French doors to the balcony were open and he imagined he could hear the sound of the surf. A light came from the partially opened doorway to the bathroom. He rolled toward the nightstand and looked at the clock. Just after two o'clock in the morning. They'd slept perhaps five hours, considering the time they'd taken to have Chinese food delivered, which they'd eaten out of cartons in bed.

Travis smiled, stretched his arms over his head and smiled again. He felt great. On top of the world. He'd done the right thing in coming to California. Maybe Jodie shouldn't have run away from Texas, but maybe he shouldn't have ridden out to the spring after their argument at the house. He should have been more understanding, more willing to listen.

Which is exactly what Hank had pointed out. Travis hadn't really looked at arguments in an analytical way before since he always avoided verbal warfare, but Hank had pointed out that when a person wasn't too concerned over who was right, they could get a lot more accomplished. Travis had been sure he was right about Jodie focusing too much on her career. Now he was doing his best to see the situation from her point of view. He hoped that she could do the same thing for him.

She appeared in the doorway, silhouetted by the light. Damn, she looked good. She'd dressed in some sort of short, silky robe. He could clearly see her figure through the thin material and the image made his previously sated body rise to attention.

"Care to join me in the whirlpool tub?" she asked. "When I left my meetings, I thought all I wanted was a long soak in the tub and to watch the sunset from my balcony. But then you were here and I changed my mind."

He rolled to the edge of the bed, sat there and ran a hand through his unruly hair. "Do you always take a bath in the middle of the night?"

"Only when a certain cowboy makes me all hot and sweaty."

He smiled as he walked toward her. "Oh, yeah? Just one?"

"Just you," she said, reaching for him.

He walked her backward as he kissed her deeply. When she came up against the tub, he raised his head and smiled. "We got a slow start on the honeymoon, but, sweetheart, we're making up for it real fast."

Chapter Sixteen

Jodie hit the alarm clock snooze button as quickly as possible when the darn thing went off. She'd barely remembered to set it after her late night whirlpool escapade with Travis. But she had more meetings today and a dinner tonight with the cosmetics company V.P. She couldn't afford to be late.

"Don't tell me you're getting up," Travis murmured, his voice muffled by the pillow. "It's still the middle of the night."

"No, actually it's 7:00 a.m." She reached over and kissed his cheek. Yup. In the morning light, she was still in love. "Go back to sleep. There's no reason for you to get up this early."

"Why are you up?"

"I have to be back in L.A. this morning."

He propped himself up on his elbow and squinted at her. "You're working?"

"Meetings," she clarified.

He closed his eyes for a moment and she thought he was going to start arguing with her again. But then he yawned and asked, "Do you want me to drive into L.A. with you?" He rubbed her arm and reached for her fingers, covering her hand with his. He had very nice hands.

"No, there's no reason to come to the city when I can't spend time with you. Unless, of course, you just want to see the sights. Play tourist."

He shook his head, then fell silent. In a moment he asked, "When will you be back? We still have a lot to talk about."

"I'm sorry, but I'll probably be late. I have to go to dinner tonight with one of the V.P.s and the advertising executives who'll be handling the account." She pushed herself from the bed before she was tempted to stay.

"I'll miss you, Jodie."

"I'll miss you, too." She stretched, thinking of the long boring day ahead. This was one of those meetings where they needed to see her more than she wanted to see them. "Hey, I have an idea. Why don't you come to dinner with us tonight? We won't be talking too much business and they'll get a chance to meet you."

"They're okay with the marriage?"

"Oh, yes. I got so many 'best wishes' and 'congratulations' and jokes that we barely got any work done for the first half hour. They'd read about the wedding in the papers and saw footage of us in Ranger Springs on the entertainment shows."

"If you're sure you want me to come into L.A., I'll be glad to go to dinner."

"Yes, this will be great. We can spend some time together and they'll get to know you. Do you want me to send a car service for you?"

"No, I'll make arrangements. Don't worry about me."

She almost readily said, *I won't,* but knew that sounded flippant. She had confidence in Travis's ability to navigate in a different city, to find the restaurant and dress properly for dinner without her input. As a matter of fact, he'd shown himself to be a very take-charge kind of guy.

The alarm sounded again and she snatched it up quickly. "I'm sorry again. I'm going to take a shower and get ready. Go back to sleep if you'd like."

"Don't forget to leave me the name of the restaurant and what time you want me there."

"I won't," she said before she disappeared into the bathroom.

She needed to get away from Travis before she gave in to the temptation to crawl back into bed. Back into his arms. Sleeping and making love all day long sounded much too good right now.

"Jodie?"

She peered around the door facing into the fuzzy morning light of the bedroom. "Yes?"

"Are we going to tell them about the baby tonight?"

Her heart raced as though she were having a panic attack. Which, of course, she wasn't. He'd simply asked a valid question.

"No, I don't think so. It's not the right time and probably not the right place, either."

"I thought perhaps it would be easier with me beside

you. We have to tell them soon, especially if they're building a long-term ad campaign around you."

"I know, and I will tell them soon. But not yet."

Travis didn't say anything else. She loosened her grip on the door facing and retreated into the bathroom.

TRAVIS HAD A BAD FEELING about this evening as he pulled his rental car under the busy hotel portico in L.A. He hadn't heard from Jodie all day and he knew she had to be exhausted. They'd gotten very little sleep after he'd joined her in the whirlpool tub. Just a nap, really, of a couple of hours before her alarm had gone off. He'd been incredulous that she was getting up at all since she hadn't mentioned today's schedule yesterday or this morning.

She didn't need to be in meetings so soon after having a medical scare. She should be home with her feet propped up, taking care of herself and their baby. Even if she was just sitting around all day at a conference table, she would be tired. And now they were going out to eat. If he could, he'd whisk her away from this crazy California lifestyle and back to Texas where she'd be safe and relaxed until after the baby was born. But that kind of action had gotten him into trouble before, so he was going to tamp down his basic instincts.

He wasn't sure when he'd gotten so protective of women. He only knew that he felt an obligation to Jodie to keep her healthy, especially since she showed such disregard for her own well-being.

With a sigh, he pocketed his valet claim check, exited the Lincoln and straightened his jacket lapels. He hadn't been sure what he should wear, so he'd done a little shopping in upscale Newport Beach after arranging for a rental car. Jodie had offered to send a car service to pick him up, but he didn't feel right doing that. A real Texan didn't get himself stranded without "wheels" in a strange town.

The restaurant they'd chosen was in a large hotel, so he entered the lobby and located the signature, nearly unintelligible black script on a brass plaque. Like a lot of things in California, the sign looked pretentious.

He saw Jodie immediately at the bar, surrounded by three avidly attentive men of different ages and looks. One was middle-aged, paunchy and balding; the short one was younger, with an athlete's build; the third one was a studious, thirty-ish African-American. She shone as though a spotlight had been placed overhead to show off her blond hair and luminescent skin. After a long day of meetings, she still looked radiant. Only he seemed to sense how hard she was working to appear relaxed.

The very idea that she had to entertain and enthrall these men made him angry all over again.

Waving off the maître d', Travis strode to the group. "Sweetheart, I hope I didn't keep you waiting," he said, placing his arm around her shoulders.

She smiled and leaned against him, as though she were absorbing his strength. He was glad to share. He would gladly shoulder her burdens if only she'd allow him into her life. Perhaps after last night…

"No, we got finished a few minutes early and came on over to the restaurant. Let me introduce you," she said, straightening but not stepping away from his arm.

"Norm Edwards, Mitch Reynolds and Jamal Mitchell, this is my husband, Travis Whitaker."

The three men congratulated him and shook his hand, which he endured for Jodie's sake. What he really wanted to do was to walk her out of the restaurant, to the registration desk, then into a hotel room, where she could slip between some cool sheets with him and sleep for about ten hours—after which he'd make to love to her until they were both exhausted but sated.

He motioned for the maître d' and soon they were escorted to their table. Jodie sank into the chair, then almost immediately straightened and pasted a smile on her face.

"The stuffed mushrooms here are fantastic," she said.

"Let's have a round of drinks first to celebrate," Norm Edwards said, nodding toward the waiter.

Everyone ordered their mixed drink of choice. Jamal turned to Jodie. "Your usual lemon drop martini?" he asked.

"No, not tonight," she said.

"Oh, come on, Jodie. Have a drink with us," Mitch urged. He looked up at the waiter. "Bring the lady—"

"She's not having her usual tonight," Travis said, ready to punch the guy if he continued to be so pushy. *Tell them you're pregnant*, he silently urged Jodie. *This is your chance.*

"You know that alcohol can make your skin age. You

wouldn't want me to look all wrinkled and sallow in the photos, would you?"

"You'll never look wrinkled and sallow," Norm said.

"Right," Jamal added. "You'll be the girl next door for a long, long time."

"Just the same, I'm passing on the martini. Bring me a bottle of Pellegrino, please," she told the waiter.

They received their drinks and talked shop, which pretty much left him sipping a Chivas and water, watching Jodie and wondering how long this dinner would last.

They devoured crab-stuffed mushrooms, smoked salmon on endive and another round of drinks before ordering dinner. Travis shifted in his chair, glanced at his watch and continued to sip his first scotch and water. Jodie had been gone from her condo for twelve hours, way too long, in his opinion. She needed to take better care of herself now, not when it was convenient to her career.

"Will you be moving to California, Travis?" Jamal asked as the main course was cleared away.

"No. I'm a Texan, through and through." *As their child would be,* he silently vowed.

"Then, Jodie, are you moving to Texas?"

"Well, of course I'll be with my husband," she said, wrapping her hand around his bicep and smiling broadly. "I'll also keep my condo in Newport Beach, and I'll be traveling to New York or wherever I need to go. Travis understands about my schedule."

No, he doesn't, Travis felt like saying. Instead he smiled and placed his hand over hers. "Hopefully, Jodie

will grow to love Texas as much as I do," he said to the
men at the table—and especially to his reluctant wife.

"The town is very charming. I've already made some
friends there."

"I'm sure they're quite impressed to have a world-
famous model marrying into their community."

"No, I don't think—"

"Yes, I'll bet you really stand out among all those
cowgirls," Norm said with an annoying chuckle.

"They like Jodie for who she is, not what she does
for a living," Travis contradicted.

"Still, a small town like that…" Mitch said.

"Like what?" Travis narrowed his eyes and glared at
the executive. The hell with being polite for Jodie's
sake. These yahoos were disparaging his town.

"I'm sure this Rancher Falls is nice—"

"Ranger Springs," he corrected Jamal.

Norm waved off his comment. "They should be
lucky Jodie is putting them on the map."

"They kind of got on the map when one of the local
girls married the most eligible bachelor in Europe. You
might have heard of Prince Alexi of Belegovia."

"Oh, that's right. I remember now. Well, what a co-
incidence. Now the town has a European princess and
an American princess."

"I'm not a princess."

"No, you're the girl next door!" Norm exclaimed.
"Let's have a round of drinks to toast the Girl Next
Door ad campaign."

"Let's not," Travis muttered under his breath. He was

getting really tired of these guys. If Jodie had to put up with these nitwits to make a living, maybe she would be better off living in a small town.

No, he shouldn't think that. He understood that she loved her career. She'd just achieved everything she'd been working for, and as she'd told him, she wouldn't be a fresh, young face forever. But dammit, she should have more than a portfolio of photographs and a legacy of commercials. She should have a family who loved her in a community who appreciated her for who she was. She should have a husband who loved her…

He looked at her, the bigger-than-life woman with the glowing skin and gilded hair, the sparkling green eyes now dulled with fatigue. He loved being with her—and had from the very first moment they'd met. She intrigued and excited him more than any other woman he'd known. Certainly more than those insipid airheads he'd dated ever since Tiffany had walked out of his life. He also loved the way she looked, how she felt when he held her and made love to her. How she made him feel when they were alone and she reached for him.

My God, he'd fallen in love with his wife!

"This has been great," he told the three men who were avidly listening to their waiter describe the tray of desserts, "but we've had a long day. It's time for us to say good-night." He linked his hand with Jodie's and pulled her to her feet.

"But we haven't talked about sight-seeing tomorrow," Mitch complained.

"Or the schedule for the next round of meetings in New York," Jamal added.

"Sorry, guys. Jodie needs her rest and as her husband, I'm going to see that she gets it. Good night."

"I'll talk to you tomorrow," she said tightly to the men as she reached down for her purse.

"What about my car?" she asked as they walked toward the exit.

"You won't need it tonight, and I'll bring you in tomorrow to pick it up."

They didn't speak as they waited for his car to be brought around. He didn't trust his voice or his mood in public. That odd protectiveness he'd felt since Jodie had arrived at his house was back with a passion. He needed to get her alone so he could tell her about his realization.

But when they were finally alone and he pulled out of the portico onto the still busy streets of L.A., she turned to him and asked, "Who do you think you are to interfere with my career?"

JODIE FINALLY KNEW the meaning of the word "livid." If she hadn't been wearing a seat belt and if Travis hadn't been driving a car, she would have grabbed two handfuls of his Hugo Boss jacket and shaken him until his perfect white teeth rattled. The nerve of that man, practically dragging her out of the restaurant!

"I'm your husband, in case you've forgotten since just this morning."

"You know what I mean! Those men are important to my career."

"Then maybe you should find yourself another career," he nearly growled as he turned to enter the ramp to the freeway.

"I like my career just fine, thank you very much. And I don't need help from you."

"You need someone to take care of you, since you obviously don't want to do so yourself."

"I'm just a little tired. That's perfectly understandable, given the fact I got about three hours of sleep last night."

"And that's my fault, I agree, although I wouldn't have kept you up all night if you'd bothered to tell me that you were going to be working all day today."

"You didn't give me a chance!"

"You had chances. Just a few short sentences would have done the trick. But you didn't want me to know, did you, Jodie? You wanted to get up and slip out of the house and never tell me that your precious career meant more than our marriage."

"That's completely unfair! I've never compared our marriage and my career. You're the one who keeps weighing the two."

"Well, maybe you should start comparing them."

"What do you mean by that?"

"Just what I said. You need to decide what is more important to you, our marriage and the baby we created together, or the career you've already built."

"Are you giving me an ultimatum?" she asked incredulously. *Who did he think he was?*

"Yeah, I guess maybe I am."

"Ask anyone. I don't react well to ultimatums."

"Dammit, Jodie, you don't react well to anything I've asked. You won't slow down, you won't put this pregnancy first and you damned well won't give our marriage a chance. I can't go on like this."

"You're being unreasonable! I can't give up my career just because I'm pregnant. I shouldn't be expected to give up my life just because I got married."

Travis stared at her, his eyes cold in the green light of the car's instrument panel. Her heartbeat and rapid breathing filled the car with a type of panicky energy she couldn't control. He was so silent that she wondered if he would say anything to her…and she wasn't sure she wanted him to. She was tired of fighting him, tired of defending her choices. Just…tired.

"Why did you marry me, Jodie?"

"I told you why. I needed to get married because of the contract. It's everything I've worked for, everything I've wanted."

"I understand that, but I told you my terms. A real marriage. Not a temporary legal arrangement so you could salvage your career."

"Yes, I know, but…"

"But you didn't really mean it, did you?"

"I meant it. I tried, but you always want more."

"Why do you think that is?"

She threw up her hands. "I have no idea!"

"Well, why don't you think about it," he said as he put the car into gear and prepared to merge into traffic.

She sat on her side of the car, as close to the door as

possible, and tried to ignore his cold presence. How could a man as giving and passionate as Travis be so cold to her now? Didn't he care for her at all? No, he probably hated her. She was an inconvenience, a burden that he'd been saddled with.

Just like her father, who hadn't wanted the responsibility of raising two daughters. He'd valued his freedom too much to be a dad to her and her sister. Her sister had never really recovered from his rejection, but Jodie believed she'd done a good job of moving on. She didn't blame her father for not wanting his children.

But she wanted this baby. She wanted Travis, too, but she didn't know how to have him in her life. He didn't even approve of her life! He might want her in *his* life, but she wasn't a small-town girl from Texas. She couldn't be shuffled away to his ranch so she could be coddled and protected for the next seven months. She didn't want that type of treatment from any man, especially a man who had seemed to treat her as an equal and had respected her independence when they'd first met.

Travis had asked—make that, ordered—that she think about why he was acting this way. But he hadn't given her any clues, and now her head was pounding and her stomach was churning, and all she wanted to do was to go home and fall into bed.

"I don't understand you," she said, barely above a whisper. "All I know is that I don't want to argue with you tonight. I'm too tired to think."

"I know you are, Jodie, and that's why you should

be home, resting. But you won't listen to me, so I'm going back to Texas."

"We should get this resolved, Travis. You can't just keep running away from me when you don't like what I say."

"I'm not running away. I'm leaving you in peace, because my presence seems more upsetting than my absence."

"It's not always easy to establish a relationship." She leaned back against the headrest and thought of her single mother, because that was easier than facing her husband's immediate departure. Despite what he'd claimed, he was running away to Texas.

Which she supposed, deep down inside, made her think of the father who had deserted his family so many years ago that she hardly remembered him.

Her mother hadn't needed a man in her life. There had been no stepfather for Jodie and her sister, and there hadn't been any "uncles" spending the night, either. Had her mother remained single because getting along with a man was just too darn hard?

All Jodie knew for sure was that she'd grown up believing that a woman could depend only on herself, even when she loved her family and they loved her.

She couldn't depend on Travis. He'd certainly never said he loved her, and she wasn't about to admit her weakness for his handsome face, great body and mostly caring personality. If only he weren't so protective and possessive. She didn't need protecting, and she darn sure wasn't a possession.

"Maybe it would be best if you returned to Texas. I'll be there in a few days."

"Are you sure you can work it into your schedule?"

She turned and glared at him. "Look, I'm trying to make this work."

"Are you, Jodie? Or are you just trying to make this look like a real marriage for those people you work with?"

Chapter Seventeen

The drive back to the condo became even more tense after that. Jodie leaned against the passenger side door and closed her eyes, letting the miles pass by, letting words remain unspoken. She felt the burning sting of tears that she wouldn't shed and the churning sensation of the rich dinner she'd barely eaten. She wanted to get back home, huddle in her bed and listen to the sound of the distant surf drifting through her windows.

No, what I really want is to cuddle up with Travis, let him protect me and keep me safe. I want to know he's possessive because he cares about me as a person. I want to know he loves me.

But he didn't love her, and the way they'd botched their marriage, he never would.

"We're here," he said, his voice flat.

She opened her eyes and stirred, stiff and tense and half sick at her stomach.

"Are you okay?"

"I'm fine." She forced herself to unwind her legs, unwrap her arms from where they were clutched around her middle, and open the door. The smell of surf and the cool night air comforted her.

"I'll get my luggage and head for the airport."

"You don't have to. You can wait until the morning if you'd like."

"I don't think that's a good idea."

She leaned against the door. "I'm not trying to run you off. That's not what I want."

"What's happening between us isn't what either one of us wants, but it's happening anyway, and I don't know how to stop it."

She closed her eyes, feeling her stomach churning again. *I don't, either,* she felt like shouting, but she didn't. Yelling wouldn't do any good. Besides, a neighbor might be taking a late-night walk or a tabloid reporter might be lurking in the bushes. How would that look in next week's rags?

Girl Next Door Yells Like A Fishwife At Estranged Husband. Wonderful publicity. Almost as good as Girl Next Door Pregnant With Texan's Love Child.

"Jodie?"

"I'm fine." She removed her key and walked toward the condo. *I'll be fine just as soon as I sleep for about twelve hours...and find a way to forget about how I feel about you,* she added silently as she stopped in front of her door.

Ten minutes later Travis left her condo, asking her to call if she had any more medical problems or needed him to make another appearance. Unlike the passionate, warm man who had made love to her yesterday, this one was polite and distant. She promised she would, calmly closed the door, and threw a Lalique glass vase into her stark white, cold fireplace.

TRAVIS TRIED THROWING himself into his next job the morning after catching the red-eye to Austin, but his heart wasn't in the concrete, nickel-plated, steel-and-glass structure. He couldn't stop seeing Jodie's face when he'd said goodbye. She'd looked so strong, yet so vulnerable inside. He'd wanted to fold her into his arms, but that keeping-her-safe urge was what got him into trouble. She insisted she didn't want to be protected, but her expression told him she did.

Maybe she didn't know herself as well as she pretended. Maybe this strong woman of the world, this "I can do anything" mentality was just a device to keep her from being vulnerable, which she obviously viewed as a weakness.

He would force himself to give her time, he vowed. He'd stop rushing her, which he had to admit he'd done ever since she'd shown up on his doorstep just days before their marriage. He'd try his best to develop some patience—never his strong suit—and not go after her.

She'd come to him when she was ready. He had to believe that, because in spite of their differences, he loved her.

AT FIVE MINUTES PAST eleven the next morning, just as Jodie was imagining lunch in bed, followed by a deep-tissue massage, the room began to spin and she slid out of her chair onto the conference room floor.

"Jodie! Oh, my God. What's wrong?" Jamal asked as he knelt beside her.

Strange how she could see him, but she didn't have the strength to answer. Or to move. She just wanted to lie here on the conference room floor and watch the acoustic tile spin slowly overhead.

"Don't move her," Mitch ordered. "We don't know what's wrong."

"I almost fainted," she whispered.

"What can we get for you, Jodie?" Jamal asked. "Do you want water?"

I want to go home, she thought. *I want to go to Travis. He'd know what to do.* He'd pick her up and carry her to bed. He'd get a wet washcloth and put it over her eyes, and then he'd call Dr. Amy, who'd come out to the ranch and take care of her.

"Call an ambulance," Norm ordered.

Now that got her attention. She didn't want an ambulance. She didn't want to go to the hospital.

"No," she whispered, then decided she wasn't getting their attention. She focused all her energy and nearly shouted. "No ambulance. I'll be fine."

"Do you have a doctor we can call? For heaven's sake, Jodie, you're scaring us to death."

She didn't want to be around men who were scared. She wanted Travis. But he was a long way away. He'd left her because she wouldn't let him take care of her, and now that she needed him, he was gone. Tears welled in her eyes as she turned her head to the side and closed her eyes. "Call my mother," she said. "Travis had to go back to Texas."

"You need to go to the hospital and get checked. It's not normal to faint."

"It is when you're pregnant," she whispered, then realized what she'd said. She'd told them her secret, weeks before she'd planned.

"You're pregnant?" Jamal practically shouted.

"Mmm-hmm," she said. "Not very far along, but I'm going to have a baby. In the fall."

"This could change everything!" Norm exclaimed.

"Jodie, are you sure?" Mitch asked.

"I'm sure," she said softly. "I'm going to have a baby. And I want my mother." *I really want my husband, but he left me.* Instead of admitting that bit of information, she gave them her mother's office number and her cell phone number.

"Are you sure you shouldn't go to the hospital?"

"I'm sure. I think I just got hungry. I didn't eat enough breakfast. And I'm tired."

"You need to take it easy," Jamal stated.

"Yes, I think I've heard that before," she replied, smiling as she remembered the bossy way Travis had told her to slow down, to take it easy. She hadn't taken his advice, and now she was lying on the conference room floor, scaring the heck out of three grown men.

Too bad the female members of the team were working on the photos taken two days ago. They'd at least know to get her a wet towel and maybe some orange juice. Or even Neil, who could be a bit fussy but really cared about her. Of course, he couldn't pick her up as Travis had done. No one was as strong and sure as her absent husband.

By the time her mother arrived, Jodie was resting on the couch in Norm's office, sipping orange juice. She looked up into the worried face and felt the tears well up again. This time she didn't try to stop them.

"What's wrong, baby?" her mother asked, rushing in then kneeling beside the couch.

"I've really screwed up this time," Jodie said, reaching out and holding her mother tight. "And I want to go home. Home to Travis."

TRAVIS GOT A CALL on his cell phone while he, Hank and Greg Rafferty were sitting at Schultze's Roadhouse at dinner. Greg's wife, Carole, was attending one of those women-only parties for decorations or plastic bowls or something with Gwendolyn and a lot of other women in town. The two displaced husbands had joined Travis for the evening. Mostly they were talking about the joys of married life while he sipped his third beer and tried not to worry about Jodie.

He looked at the number before answering, his heart racing as he noticed the Los Angeles area code. "Jodie?"

"No, this is her mother."

"Mrs. Marsh. What's wrong?"

"Jodie had a fainting spell during one of her meetings today, just before noon. I think it was just a little low blood sugar. By the time she got to the doctor, she was back to normal."

He sat up straighter and ran a hand through his hair. The buzz he'd so carefully nursed for the past hour disappeared in a rush of adrenaline. *I knew this was going to happen,* he felt like shouting. The reality was far worse than he'd imagined. Especially now that he was over a thousand miles away, drinking beer with his friends while his wife lay in bed in California.

"So she's okay now? She didn't hurt herself or…or anything?"

"You mean, the baby? No, the baby is fine. Jodie's okay now. She just felt a little faint. I don't think she actually lost consciousness."

"Where is she now?"

"She's at my house in Orange, but she wants to come home."

"Home to her condo?" he asked as his pulse pounded heavily against the cold metal of his phone.

"No, she wants to come to Texas."

Travis closed his eyes and said a short prayer of thanks. "I'll come and get her."

"Travis, there's no reason for you to fly out here. She wants to come back to Ranger Springs as soon as possible."

"But she shouldn't be alone."

"What's wrong?" Hank asked.

Travis tilted the phone away from his mouth. "It's Jodie. She fainted and she wants to come home."

Hank and Greg exchanged a look, but Travis didn't want to take the time to explain to them what he was talking to Jodie's mother about.

"How soon can she travel? What did the doctor say?"

"Well, they'd rather she waited a while, but she's pretty intent on leaving as soon as she can get a flight."

"She needs to be careful! I know I keep telling her that, but—" He paused and ran his hand through his hair again. "Wait a minute. How come *she* didn't call me? Are you sure she's okay?"

"She's sleeping. She said she didn't sleep much last night after you left. After she had a meal she was tired, but as soon as she wakes up I know she'll try to get a flight out."

"Travis, I think I have a solution," Greg said.

"Just a minute, Mrs. Marsh." Travis put his hand over the mouthpiece. "What?"

"Carole and I flew down on our family's corporate jet. I can have it sent out to California for Jodie. That way she doesn't have to worry about schedules, and she can rest comfortably on the flight."

"That sounds great, Greg. I hadn't even thought about leasing a jet yet. My head is still swimming from the idea that she fainted. I knew she was pushing herself too hard, but I took the easy way out and left her in California."

"Don't beat yourself up over it. You know how head-strong women are."

He removed his hand from the mouthpiece. "Mrs. Marsh, Greg Rafferty is sending the Huntington Foods' jet to L.A. to get Jodie." To bring her home. "I'm going to be on that plane."

"That's good, Travis. She needs you."

"Did she say that?"

"No, not exactly, but she said she wanted to go home to you. Jodie is very independent and it's difficult for her to rely on anyone else."

"I know. Thank you for calling…and for taking care of her."

"It was my job first," Mrs. Marsh said with a bit of amusement and irony in her voice.

He ended the call after getting information about the closest airport and Mrs. Marsh's address. Then he turned to his friends. "I'm going to get my wife."

"I'll take care of things at the ranch," Hank said.

"I'll call for the jet to be ready," Greg offered.

"You two are the best. If we have a boy, I guess I'm going to have to name him after you two."

"What?" they both shouted in unison.

"Maybe I shouldn't rush back to Texas," Jodie said, hugging the pillow to her chest.

"Too late," her mother said. "I've already called your husband. He's coming to get you in a private jet."

"What!" Jodie sat up straight and dropped the pillow.

Her mother sank down on the bed. "Jodie, when you were feeling so bad, the one person you wanted—more than your mother, of course—was your husband. You said you wanted to go home to Texas. Now he's coming to get you. Isn't that what you really want?"

"Oh, Mom, I'm just not sure."

Her mother pushed a strand of blond hair behind Jodie's ear. "I think what you mean is that you're afraid."

Jodie picked up the pillow again. "Okay, I'm afraid. But you don't understand. When I met Travis, it was 'bam,' and we had this wonderful weekend, and then we both went back to our real worlds. And we didn't fool each other. We promised we only wanted that weekend."

"But?" her mother prompted.

"But I did think about him. A lot. Guys like Travis don't come along every day. And then there was that fantastic chemistry."

"Please, don't go into so much detail that you make your mother cringe."

Jodie managed a weak smile. "I really was going to honor our mutual agreement and not pursue a relationship."

"But then you discovered you were pregnant."

"I couldn't very well be the 'knocked-up girl next door,' could I?"

Her mother smiled. "No, you couldn't."

"So I went to Texas and asked Travis to marry me."

Her mother settled more comfortably on the mattress. "Tell me, Jodie, did you think this marriage you proposed was permanent? Or was it only for the baby?"

"Well, really, it was for my career."

"So you had no other reason?"

"Mom, all I could think about was that contract I'd just signed. The morality clause I'd agreed to. If they knew I'd had unprotected sex with someone I'd just met—"

Her mother held up her hand. "Please, this is your mother. Not so much detail."

"Geesh, how did you think I got pregnant?"

"I'm trying not to think about it." Her mother paused, then asked, "So, now that you've been married for a while, how do you feel about Travis?"

Jodie leaned back against the headboard. "I love him, but—"

"But what?"

"He's...difficult."

"Jodie, did I raise you to beat around the bush like this? What's so difficult about loving your husband?"

"He wants to surround me in a plastic bubble. I think he'd be happy if I'd stay home, lie around and eat organic food for the next seven months. It's as if he's scared that my regular life is *dangerous*. I do not lead a dangerous life!"

"No, but you are very active and...well, sometimes you are a little too confident."

"How can I be too confident? Are you saying I'm reckless?"

"No, but you're a natural optimist. You think everything's going to be fine. No problems. Don't worry, be happy. That's rather upsetting to someone who's concerned about you—and the baby, of course. It's especially hard if that person is in love with you."

"Travis never told me he's in love with me. Before I came to him with our problem, he'd vowed to never marry."

"Then he must have feelings for you to change his mind."

"Maybe he just felt pushed into it. Maybe he wants the baby, but he doesn't necessarily want a wife. Or at least he didn't think he wanted one a couple of weeks ago."

"Obviously he changed his mind. And I don't believe for a minute that he only wants the baby. You might not have noticed how that man looks at you, but believe me, he's not thinking about babies."

"Okay, so he lusts after me. I already knew that."

"I'm not talking about lust, although I know that's important, too. No, I think Travis is in love with you. He has all the symptoms."

"You make it sound like a communicable disease."

"Well, you've both caught it, haven't you?"

"I don't know!" Jodie threw up her hands in frustration, dropping the pillow to her lap. "How can I be sure? What if I go to Texas and he's just demanding that I give up my career? I've worked too hard for too long to sit around his house and eat bonbons for the next seven months."

"Did he ask you to quit work?"

"Not exactly. But he doesn't understand. If I don't co-operate, if they have to redo the schedules or push back the launch date, I'll cost them money and get a reputation as being difficult."

"Did they tell you this?"

"No, they don't have to. I know how this business works. They could drop me!"

"Can you be replaced that easily?"

"Well, I—I don't know. Maybe. I'm not getting any younger."

"I don't think they'll find another Jodie Marsh. You're unique, honey, and you're only twenty-nine. You provide a very specific image they're looking for—the average, ideal woman. Plus you have a reputation for being genuinely nice. Do you think they'll push you aside if you have to juggle your schedule a little?"

Jodie closed her eyes and rubbed her temples. "I don't know, Mom."

"Why don't you talk to them? Ask them for a few days off, and go back to Texas. You know you want to. He was the one you wanted first. Go with him. See if he's your destiny. You can always go back to your career."

"What if they don't want me back? What if Travis isn't right for me? I'll be left with nothing."

"No, you wouldn't. You'd still have yourself, and me and your sister. And others who love you. Soon you'll have a baby, too." Her mother paused and smoothed Jodie's hair back from her forehead. "Do you want Travis because you're afraid to be alone?"

"No, of course not."

"Then what are you afraid of?"

She started to say something like "I'm not afraid," but she'd already admitted that she was afraid of his rejection, his...desertion.

"I tried so hard to be independent. I practically pushed him away by focusing on my career, my schedule, my needs. But he didn't go away until yesterday, when I pushed too hard."

"I think you have to ask yourself why it's so important for you to be independent of your husband."

"You taught me to be independent! You always said that if a woman has her own education, career and money, she can make many more choices than someone who's dependent on a man. And look at Chelsea! She flits from one man to another like a hungry sparrow."

"That's not a very nice analogy," her mother said.

"Okay, I'm sorry, but you know what I mean. She's not independent. She depends on men for everything."

"Yes, and I'm not advocating you become more like your sister. She makes her own choices and, granted, some of them aren't very good. But Jodie, Travis isn't just another man. He's your husband. The father of your child."

"What about your husband, Mom? My father. He didn't stick around. You couldn't depend on him."

"No, I couldn't, but that doesn't mean you can't depend on Travis. That doesn't mean you can't love him as much as I wanted to love your father at one time. I never got that great love of my life, Jodie, but you can. As a matter of fact, I think everything you want is just within your reach." She smoothed Jodie's hair back again. "Don't be afraid to go for what you want, baby. Travis isn't like your father, and you're not me. We all have to follow our own dreams. I think yours is more complicated, but that doesn't mean you can't have everything you want."

"Do you think?" Jodie asked in a small voice that she could barely coax past her tight throat.

"Yes, I think so," he mother said, smiling in that all-knowing way that Jodie had depended on all her life.

She didn't have a father to love, but she had an extraordinary mother. She had a wonderful role model. Now she needed to go beyond what her mother had shown her by example. She needed to reach out to the man she'd fallen in love with.

But, oh, the idea was so frightening. Could they compromise on her career and make a future together? Or, like her mother, was she destined to be a single mom, a woman without the love of her life?

Chapter Eighteen

Travis couldn't wait for the jet to touch down at the private airport just miles from Orange, where Jodie's mother lived. As soon as the steps were unfolded, he paced to the door, said a quick thanks to the pilot and hit the pavement. If his rental car was waiting as he'd arranged, he would see her in less than a half hour.

His heart pounded as though he'd run all the way from Texas. So much depended on what he said and did. He wanted to convince her to slow down, but he also needed to listen to her...if only she'd talk to him. If only she'd tell him why her career was so important that she'd risked her health.

I'm a man on a mission, he told himself as he strode through the night toward the well-lit terminal. *A mission to make my wife love me.* Minutes later, he was behind the wheel of a new Lincoln, his map to Jodie's mother's house spread out beside him on the seat. He fought the darkness and the traffic, negotiating the streets to find the right turnoff. At last he located her street, breathing a sigh of relief when he saw the pale yellow bungalow with yucca plants and various flowers planted along the concrete walk from the narrow driveway, just as it had been described to him. The porch lights and outdoor lighting made the house easy to see in the unfamiliar neighborhood.

Behind the sheer curtains, he saw someone pacing. Jodie or her mother? He couldn't tell from this angle on the drive. All he knew was that he needed to be inside that house, bringing his wife home to Texas.

Still, he felt as though he were wearing lead boots as he walked up the steps and rang the doorbell.

And then she opened the door.

"Jodie," he whispered hoarsely. He coughed, then said, "How are you?"

"I'm okay. I feel fine now."

"Good, that's good," he said, his lead feet anchoring him to the porch.

"Travis, you didn't have to come. I was going to come to you."

"Were you?"

"I… Yes, I was. I did have some second thoughts. I had some…issues."

"And now?"

"We need to talk. Come inside," she said, stepping back from the doorway.

He stepped from the porch into the small foyer, reluctantly looking away from Jodie to the tastefully decorated living room. Jodie's mother was neat and obviously partial to a soothing shade of light green. "Where is your mother?"

"She's out back on the patio. She wanted to give us a place to talk."

He wished he held a hat in his hands. Or something to keep from grabbing Jodie, pulling her close and kissing her until they both couldn't breathe. The urge to hold her was so strong, he resisted the impulse only by reminding himself that this was her mother's house. They weren't alone, and besides, just this morning Jodie had almost passed out.

"Your mother scared five years off my life when she called earlier."

Jodie laced her fingers together as she stood just inside the living room. "I'm sorry. I really was going to call you, but she beat me to it."

"I'm glad she called." He took a step forward. "I wanted to be with you."

"But you'd just left me."

He took a deep breath. "You know why I couldn't stay. We talked about it." He took two more steps into the room, stopping in front of her, beside the chintz sofa.

"You did most of the talking, the explaining, last night. I didn't really know what to say."

He sat on the sofa, took her hands and urged her down beside him. "Jodie, we need to be honest with each other. We need to communicate."

"I know," she said, searching his eyes, reading his expression. "But I was too surprised and too afraid to tell you how I was feeling last night."

"Just last night, or feeling about us in general?"

"Travis, I don't think there's anything 'in general'

about us. Everything is immediate and intense and frightening."

"Frightening?"

"Haven't you felt it, too? Aren't you a little scared by what's happening?"

"No. At first I was…reluctant. I thought I knew what I wanted from life. I have a great career, a new house in a town that feels like it's been home forever and enough money to travel anywhere I want to go. I had a little black book with enough names and numbers of cute, superficial women who didn't make demands on me."

"So you had it all," she stated.

"No, I didn't. I just thought I did. I was never really happy," he said, taking both her hands, "until I stood beside the exam table and watched Dr. Amy make a picture of our baby on that sonogram screen. Then my life seemed to fall into place. Our life seemed full of limitless possibilities."

"But then I disappointed you. I didn't do what you thought I should."

"No, you didn't, but to be fair, I overreacted." He paused, then said, "I realized that part of my reaction was based on my mother's need to put her career above her family. She didn't want to be a has-been actress. Being a mother wasn't enough for her, and I think I confused my feelings when you seemed to place more importance on your modeling. I'm sorry I overreacted."

"Apology accepted, and I understand about your mother. Yes, you do sometimes overreact. That's your trademark. Mine is not communicating with you. I understand now how you got so frustrated with me. I was afraid to talk to you about everything. My career, our lives, our baby. I think I ran back to the life I knew because it was much more comfortable than thinking about the future."

"Why were you frightened of the future?"

"Because other than my mother, I've never been able to trust anyone besides myself. As long as I was responsible for my success or failure, I felt secure."

"You've been very successful in your career. Is there room in your life for family?"

"I'm making room." He must have appeared skeptical, because she quickly added, "No, I really am. I've already called Neil and Felicia to explain the situation. She's calling everyone tomorrow to tell them I need a week or so off, doctor's orders. Then we'll work out a new schedule."

"You're serious?"

"Completely," she said emphatically. Then she smiled and added, "It's about time, don't you think?"

"Absolutely," he said, keeping his smile until his lips touched hers. Even then, he felt so happy that he couldn't stop grinning, so he nibbled his way from her lips to her ear, then down her neck.

Soon they were both breathing hard and no longer grinning. "Damn, we're in your mother's living room, aren't we?"

"Yes, we are. But I do remember something about a private jet, don't I?"

His grin returned. "Very private. With a bedroom."

Her answering smile made his blood boil. "Let me say goodbye to Mom, then we'll go."

"Home to Texas," he said as she walked toward the patio.

"I'M NEVER GOING to be able to look Greg and Carole in the eyes again," Jodie said, snuggling against Travis as he leaned against the upholstered headboard of the cramped double bed. All she heard was the roar of the jet engines, so she assumed neither the pilot nor the co-pilot could hear noises coming from the back of the plane. Good thing. She'd been quite vocal about joining the "mile high club."

"We still have so much to talk about," she said, rubbing Travis's well-sculpted chest, trying to keep her hands from straying down the center line of his abs to the parts of him covered by a sheet.

"Well, I'm pretty much a captive audience. If you feel like talking now, I'm ready."

She took a deep breath. "My mother is a very strong person and my most influential role model. I've told you about her, but I haven't talked about my dad."

"No, you haven't. It's often the things we never talk about, though, that have the biggest impact in our lives."

"Exactly. And apparently that's the way it was with me. I didn't want to think about my father's desertion of the family. We always said we didn't need him. We never talked about him. And I guess he became this huge invisible influence in all our lives."

"What do you mean?"

"My mother became even stronger and more independent. When my sister grew up, she started going from man to man, looking for that missing part of her background—that powerful male presence most daughters take for granted."

"And you?"

Jodie breathed deeply, taking in the smell of Travis's cologne and the musty smell of good sex. "I was the oldest, the responsible one. I grew up more like my mother, except I was also bigger and heavier, a gangly kid with big feet and a woman's body by the time I was twelve. I also had a little bit of a chip on my shoulder from being the largest girl in my class. So not only did I convince myself I didn't need a man in my life, I knew that I couldn't depend on one to support me either financially or emotionally."

"That's not a bad attitude, Jodie. It's only harmful if you exclude everyone from your life who might want to support you—either financially or emotionally. It's harmful if you won't let someone in because you're convinced they will fail you."

"I know that now, but I hadn't really thought about it before I talked to my mother. She's pretty insightful."

"Oh, yeah? Did she say anything about me?"

"She thinks…well, she thinks you're in love with me."

Travis leaned around to look at her. She felt flushed and embarrassed by his quirky smile. "She does, does she?" He curved his palm around her jaw. "I think she's right."

"Oh, Travis," she whispered. Her heart overflowed with love just as her eyes filled with tears of joy. "Tell me," she said hoarsely.

"I love you, Jodie Marsh."

"I love you, too, Travis Whitaker. More than you know."

They kissed and she turned in his arms, her breasts

pressed tightly against his chest. She slid her leg higher, encountering the evidence of his renewed desire.

He broke the kiss and smiled. "What can I say? You inspire me."

"I do."

"Oh, yeah." He kissed her again, then pulled back to look into her eyes. "I know we've got the passion, but there's more to a marriage than making love. I want you to know that I'll never try to hold you back from going after what you want. I was too bossy, but I'm new at this."

"You've been married before," she reminded him.

"Yes, but I never felt this worried, this possessive before." He smiled tenderly. "I guess I should have known then that I was in love with you."

"Well," she said, running her fingers through his hair, "as long as you know it now."

"Believe me, I do. And I'm serious, Jodie. If you want to continue modeling, that's fine with me. I'll miss you terribly when you travel, but you'll always know where home is. And I promise I'll be the best father ever to our little peanut."

"Even when that means changing diapers and pacing the floor late at night?"

"Especially then. I'm going to learn everything possible about babies."

"You're going to be impossibly, obsessively exuberant about this baby, aren't you?"

"Absolutely," he said with a grin.

"Well, I forgive you in advance, as long as you don't forget the baby's mother."

"Never," he said fiercely. "I couldn't get you out of my mind after that first weekend together, and I can't get enough of you now."

She ran her leg along his thighs and smiled. "Mmm, I see. Do you think we have time for a little more mile-high activity?"

"Absolutely," he whispered before he kissed her and pressed her down into the pillows.

SEVEN MONTHS LATER, Jodie waddled out of the Four Square Café into the heat of September. "This was probably a mistake. I think I should have stayed home, sitting under a ceiling fan with my feet propped up."

"Are you feeling bad? Any problems?"

"No! And don't start telling me to be careful, either. I'm not walking fast enough to hurt myself."

Travis chuckled. "I wasn't going to tell you anything. I just thought maybe you were feeling a little closer to delivery."

"Unfortunately, your daughter isn't cooperating at all. She's as stubborn as…well, as both of us."

"She's strong-willed."

"She's also cranky."

"Like her mother."

"Hey, you'd be cranky, too, if you were carrying around a thirty-pound watermelon and couldn't see your feet."

Travis hugged her. "I'd carry our watermelon around if I could, sweetheart."

"Maybe we'll wait for modern science to give us that option before we try for the son you'd like to teach to spit."

"Hey, I was just teasing."

Jodie paused and leaned against him before getting into the SUV. "I'm sorry. I'm just so ready to see our baby."

He kissed her forehead. "It won't be long now." He paused. "Are you missing the excitement of your career? I know this past month has been hard on you, but you'll be in front of the cameras before long."

"I know," she said with a sigh. "I'm not really missing the assignments. How can I when I see my own face in all the women's magazines and even on television? But I think I will enjoy getting back into the studio—not to mention getting into some clothes that don't resemble tents."

"Maybe you should design some maternity clothes next. The swimsuits and cover-ups were big hits with the buyers."

"Maybe. At the moment I'd just like to get away from this heat."

"Let's go home and I'll try to take your mind off how miserable you are."

Jodie looked up. "What did you have in mind?"

"How about a nice cool shower?" he said with a grin.

Jodie laughed and held him as tight as she could, their nearly full-grown "peanut" pressed between them. "That's how we got into this situation to begin with."

"Yeah," he said with another big grin. "Let's go home."

That simple phrase had never sounded better.

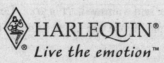

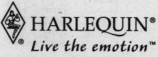